19.95

REVENGE IS BEST SERVED COLD

8/24/17

REVENGE IS BEST SERVED COLD

By

J.J. Jackson

Felony Books, a division of Olive Group, LLC,
P.O. Box 1577, Belton, MO 64012

ISBN-13: 978-1-940560-35-9

Felony Books 1st edition May 2017

10 9 8 7 6 5 4 3 2

Manufactured in the United States of America

For information regarding special discounts for bulk purchases, please contact Felony Books at felonybooks@gmail.com.

Books by Felony Books

STATUS
STATUS 2
STATUS 3
SELFIE
TRE POUND
TRE POUND 2
TRE POUND 3
THE HUSH LOVE TRILOGY
STREET MOGULS & MAFIA BOSSES
STREET MOGULS & MAFIA BOSSES 2
STREET MOGULS & MAFIA BOSSES 3
RICO
RICO 2
RICO 3
RICO 4
O.P.P.
O.P.P. 2
KEEP YO LOVE, JUST GIMME THE BAG
REVENGE IS BEST SERVED COLD
REVENGE IS BEST SERVED COLD 2
SCANDALS OF A CHI-TOWN THUG
HELL HAS NO FURY
GWOP GANG 1
GWOP GANG 2
GWOP GANG 3
TRAP-A-RELLA
TRAP-A-RELLA 2
TRAP-A-RELLA 3
TRAP-A-RELLA 4
OF MY DREAMS

and more ...

www.felonybooks.com

Author notes:

To all my prison family,

This road is a struggle for each and every one of us, but if you stay focused and love yourself first before anything else you will make it. Learn to live life no matter what your circumstances are. If you have a dream, follow it no matter what. Some can write books, music, poems, the list is endless. Whatever your talent is stick to it and press towards the mark. Nothing comes easy that is worth it. I for one know that, this has been an uphill struggle. I have to write each book by hand and hope for the best. This is why I must keep my love for each person who has supported me and been there for me from the beginning. This is what keeps me going. I know I couldn't do any of this without any of them, putting God first. Remember we must stay together and stand as one.

Keep y'all heads up and keep pushing. One.

Special Thanks:

First of all I would like to thank my Lord and Savior for giving me this creative mind and for bringing me through the storm and test of this journey. If it was not for him I would not be alive today to write and bring life to the characters of these books. Thank you God for being by my side always.

I would like to thank Kurt for being by my side and for your support in all my adventures. You have really supported me through all of this and I want you to know that I love you and I thank you for everything you do.

Thank you, Mom, you're the rock of my life and the key to my soul. You have supported me through all of this and so much more. Words can't describe the feeling I'm feeling in my heart for you. Mom, I love you so much I don't even know if the word love is strong enough. You know that you're a beautiful strong black woman. You have been mother and father and I just wanted you to know that I appreciate you in more ways than many. I RESPECT, CARE, LOVE, ADORE, AND REALLY MISS YOU, MY ROCK, MY MOM. I LOVE YOU.

My friend Calisa you are such a wonderful person with a good heart. I want you to know that you mean the world to me. You have been holding me down doing this bid and I want to thank you for not just standing beside me but standing with me. You are one of my biggest supporters. You help me each and every day to get through all of this. This has been a hard road and if I had a choice to have anyone standing with me during all of this it would always be you, my love. Thanks for accepting me into your life.

My Cornerstone Antoinette Holliday (AKA Nikki) Ba...beee if it was not for you these books would be just a dream. I can't tell you any more how much I love and appreciate your dedication and love. Girl you have been right there in making all this happen. You are, wow. I don't even have words for it. I'll just say you're more than family; you are a true friend. As a matter of fact you put the F and the D in that word friend. I have never had a friend like you and I want you to know this, when I am free there is no road that is too long for us. You have really proven that you don't have to know someone for years to be a good ass friend. Thank you so much for believing in me and giving me a chance. When I think of all of this it brings tears to my eyes. No one has ever truly believed in me like you. Nikki you are my eyes, ears, and my feet. You are the beat for my heart. From my heart I say, THANK YOU, MY FRIEND.

Tracey Estep, Wow we have come so far. Girl when we get out we will have so many laughs and so much to talk about. You will be leaving me this year but not for long. I'm right behind you. Tracey, thank you for being a shoulder to cry on. Thanks for being my encourager, my love my rock my shield you are the best is all I can say. You are wrapped up in one a jewel and masterpiece. I love you Tracey and I want you to know I'll be there for you no matter what.

Victoria Boateng, nothing fake about you. I love you so much, I love the conversations we have and the encouraging words you speak to me. When I am down you are always there to pick me up. You always have good things to say about me and you never say no. Victoria I love and admire you for your courage. We don't have far to go, but when this journey is over we will be doing bigger bigger things. Always know Victoria no matter where you are we are under one sun and I will always and remember you when I see the sun shining brightly because that is what you are in my life. I am your friend for life.

Jeidifer, (Aka Hida my prison daughter (son). LOL) Hida you are so special to me. I hold you dear in my heart. You are always there for me. No matter what you're doing, you will drop it and give me your undivided attention. Hida, you're the most appreciative person I have ever met. You are so talented and that is a good thing. You're young and you can go so far with your drawings. I know you will fulfill your dreams. Keep up the good work and know that I love you with all my heart.

Caroline Mitchell. I would like to say thank you for all the hard work you have put in these books, *Blood Lies and Tears* and *Cold as Ice*. You edited each book and did not ask for a dime. You did it from your heart and that is what makes you so special. You have been there from the beginning, holding my hand and walking me through. You never judged me. You made me stronger and I would like to say thank you. As you go on your new journey into the free world, please always remember me, as I will you. I would like to say, may the living God continue to Bless you and yours my friend. There is always a place for you in my heart.

John thank you for being there for me and for being a great support system. You are in my heart for life.

Bob H. You are such a good friend and I love you so much. You support me, and you show so much love. The fact that you are overseas and you still keep in touch, giving me hope and encouraging words is filling to my soul. I hope that we keep in touch and become untouchable friends forever.
OZ, Thank you for being in my life, and for all you have done. Thanks for your support, and your love. Keep my family and me in your prayers and continue to study God's words. I love you my friend.

Thank you, Elliot for being there, and for all your input. You're the best and thanks for the drawing of *Blood, Lies & Tears*. Love you.

Pebbles, you are such an emotional loving person with a good heart. I want you to know I appreciate you and I love you, AKA grandma for your care and support. You open your loving arms to every and any one. Even when you're down and out you still seem to find it in your heart to take care of others and give them hope when they feel like all hope is gone. Thanks so much for being there for me, you're my friend and you're a great supporter. I love you. You're a five star diva. Oh, take care of your five-star bingo hall. LOL

Pammy Cummings, Pam you are always there to support and you always give good words to me keeping me encouraged when I can't find the words for myself. Thanks for being there.

Sky, Boo you're beauty on the outside and in. I want to thank you for all the love you are showing. It really means a lot. You're the best and I love you. Big Up's to you and yours.

Sherry Washington, Girl you're so positive never hating on anyone. Your spirit is so uplifting and sweet. You always have my back and the love you show and the smile on your face, I can be feeling defeated but when I see you, you brighten up my day. Keep God first and the haters last. One.
To my Gym class, I love you all for your constant support. Keep burning those calories.

Missy Smith, Missy you are a wonderful person with a big heart. I'm happy you're in my life I shall never forget you my new hustling friend.

Wendy H., Wendy keep being funny, and thanks for all you have done for me and for your support.

Querida Lewis (AKA- Q), Q I don't know what page to put you on. The Big up's shout out, what page do I put you on? This I do know you're a good person, funny, witty, loving, caring sharing trusting and thoughtful. You need to be somebody's wom-man. LOL. Q real talk, thank you for being in my circle I love you and your spirit is the best. Keep your head up and continue to shine. One

Ashley (AKA- Ash- Bash) Thanks for your support and for having faith in my work.

D. Beverly (AKA Ms. B) Thanks for your support and for always keeping me in your thoughts and for being real. When you go home eat, eat, eat and love on the grand kids. Fatten them up. LOL

Brandi, thanks for your support and for your selflessness. You give, give and give and I know you will continue to be blessed for all you do.

Shout Out To...

Kim S, Thanks for your support.

Gina Wilson, Thanks for your support. I know you love God but you still give me support and for that I love you.

Shaquanna, (AKA- Q) You are showing some real love to all the sisters that write books. Thanks for your feedback. Thank you Q for being you.

Reds, I don't know how you do the fish bowl.

Aunt Leslie, Thanks for your help when I need it.

Rose, Tracey's bunky, thanks for reading my books.

"Big C" you stay fresh. Thanks for your support.

Marie Tate a true hustler and the biggest workaholic I know.

C.J, I just want to say I love you my friend.

Trina, thanks for your support.

To all the Alderson officers, Thanks for your support and encouraging words, when I felt like giving up you helped keep me in the game.

Thanks to all the Alderson family, Cumberland Men Camp and my prison family all over.

Big Up's To....

Donna Shebetion
Carry Hayes
Deidre Basham
Cathy Mishoe
Felicia Blake
Danielle Jones
Dawn White
Rita Johnson
Carry Hayes
Debbie Joyce
Missy Smith
Gina Wilson
Pammy Cummings
Taii Speaks
Vickey Boatain
Marie Tate
Cynthia Little
Ashley Jeter
Joy Edison
Tammy Napier
Shaquana Mack
Gloria Ogundeyi
Marlene Bossous

Thanks to all of you for your support and may the living God continue to bless you and yours.
I love you all THANKS, THANKS. THANKS!

Chapter 1

Terri

"So, Rome, this how you gon' do me?"

"Um, Terri ..."

"Don't 'um Terri' me. How you gon' come up in here wit' some hoochie momma where I party? I'm so heated right now I can't believe my boyfriend of three years is sitting in Club Luv wit' some broke down hoe."

"Who you call a hoochie momma!" the bitch says to me.

So I look at her. "I'm calling yo ass a hoochie momma. If the shoe fits, wear it!"

"C'mon Terri why it's gotta to be like that?" my boyfriend says, trying to calm me down.

"Boy please you ain't nothing! You think ,cause you gone pro, you can just do me any kinda way. Don't you?"

"Terri all I'm doing is having a drink wit' an old friend," this nigga states slyly while still sitting in his seat.

"Ok, old friend it's time for you to go," I say to this bitch nicely while staring her down.

"I ain't going nowhere. From the looks of it, Rome done moved on 'cause I'm sitting up here and yo ass is down there looking up."

See I just got a fresh weave and my nails done. I have on a $500 Prada dress and a pair of $800 Gucci shoes. This heifer gon' really make me hurt her. "Look whatever yo name is, you don't want none of this. Rome, you better tell her to mind her own business ,cause you already know..."

"He already know what?" This bitch is bold enough to stand up and ask me.

"He knows that I will whoop yo broke-down-ass!" I can't believe this hoe just cut me off, so I step back and reevaluate the situation. I know something is getting ready to pop off. If this hooker say one more thing out the side of her mouth, I'ma show her who Terri really is. I calm down, remembering where I am and who I am. I ask Rome one more time, being a lady this time. "Rome, are you gon' send her on her way or what? Is she your new piece or is she just chillin wit' you for a second or two?" By now my right eye is starting to twitch so I know I can't take much more.

"Didn't I just tell you we sitting here having a drink? Terri, you gotta remember you not my wife. You can't be telling me who I can and can't associate wit'."

Now this nigga trying to front and show off. He knows damn well when we get home he gon' be apologizing and begging for some of this good kat. Now I'm really pissed as I look at this crack-head bitch sipping on some Ace Champagne he bought. "So this is how you gon' carry it?" I ask.

"Look, how many times do he have to tell you he is wit' me, and not you. Now get..."

That did it. I leap over two steps and onto the table they are sitting at and start pounding on that bitch's face. I'm beating all hell outta of her and Rome is pulling on me, "Stop Terri, let her go, common now it ain't worth it. Let her go!"

I hear him talking, but I can't stop. I was taking out years of frustration and abuse that Rome's ass been putting me through. I raised my arm and—*Bow!*—I hit her so hard in her face my rock flew out my ring. I cut the whole left side of her face and blood is all over my white Prada dress. Rome sees he can't pull me off her so he runs around the other side of the table and tries to pull her away from the ass whooping she's getting. Security grabs me and they have my legs suspended in air but I'm still pounding on her face. I suddenly snap out of it hearing, "Let her go Terri she's unconscious, you won." I finally let her go and I look at my shaking hands. I'm still in black-out mode. I look up at Rome who's hovering over her and my anger starts to boil again. I pick up the bottle of Ace of Spades cause I'm tired of his shenanigans and—*Bow!*—I break the bottle over Rome's head.

19

I see my girl Pam running over with two glasses in her hand yelling, "Get the fuck off her, let her go!" Two guards have me pent down on the nasty floor, but I can still see Rome. He is walking around dizzmo holding the back of his head and blood is dripping down his back. All of a sudden, Pam throws the two glasses she has in her hand at the guards who have me pent on the floor. They let me go to wipe their eyes. Then Pam yells, "Run!" I get up and we haul ass out of the club. Hell, we was running so fast we forgot we had a damn car parked at the club.

When we stop running, we're at the Skylark Lounge on New York Avenue. Damn, a sista is out of breath! Pam runs in the strip club and comes out wit' our boy Mike who takes us back to my car asking no questions but are we ok. We jump in my whip and jet.

"Terri, what happened? Why was that girl out cold on the floor?" my friend since 5th grade asks me.

"Pam, I tried to hold my composure but she just wanted to keep gumming me to death. Rome's ass wasn't helping matters either. He was sitting in my face taking up for that dumb ass hoe. Pam I'm really tired, but my temper flared from all the BS Rome's been putting me through so I snapped and beat the brakes off her black dirty-looking ass."

"*Damn*, but sis..." Pam comes back. "You're 26 now, you can't be fighting and shutting down clubs no more. We ladies now." I looked at Pam feeling so ashamed 'cause she's right. That girl didn't deserve that ass whooping I just gave her, but then again I don't deserve seeing her wit' my man ever!

Chapter 2

Terri

I drop Pam off then I go back to my crib. "Damn, I see Rome beat my ass home," I say to myself when I press the garage button. OK, well I just gotta face the music. I get out the car with my bloody dress on limping to the door 'cause one of my heels broke. That shit I'm mad about, these damn shoes cost me an arm and a leg. I still don't know when I broke my heel. Was it when I was running, or in the club when I was beating that bitch's ass? That damn fight cost me a lotta damn money.

I limp in the house and I take my other shoe off and head upstairs to take a hot shower.

Out of nowhere Rome's ass approaches me yelling, "I want yo ass gone! Get yo shit and get the fuck out!"

I can't believe he's yelling this shit at me. As I stand in the hallway at the top of the stairs looking drunk, like a train just ran my ass over, all this nigga can say is get my shit and get the fuck out? So I look at his stupid ass and remind him, "Rome, we live in Maryland and according to the Maryland law you have to give my black ass 30 days' notice to move out. So until then, you can kiss my round chocolate ass. You son of a bitch!"

After telling him off, I walk my tired ass past him, go in the bathroom, turn on the shower, undress and get in. *Damn, this shower feels so good*, I think to myself while submerging my body under the water. In the background I hear rumbling coming from our bedroom, but I pay that no attention and figure that's Rome trying to get my attention or maybe his ass is packing to leave. Whichever, I'm too weak and tired to find out. I turn the water off, step out the shower, dry off and lotion my smooth coco sexy body. I slip on my Victoria Secret nightie, and spread out on our king size bed.

As I start fluffing up my pillow, here this fool comes standing over me, "So you gon' stay in my house for 30 more days?" he asks.

I'm real calm at this point 'cause a sister needs some sleep. "Rome look—I don't want to fight wit' you. So if it's a fight you looking for, go find it wit' one of your little girl toys."

"Terri, do you realize how much damage you caused tonight? That shit is gon' be all over the news tomorrow, if not tonight. I'm a basketball star and you or no one else is gon' ruin my career. My mother told me to let you go before

I went pro. Damn, I should've listened to her. A hard head makes a soft ass every time," he tells me while walking away.

I look up at his six-foot-six ass, "Rome, you and yo ghetto-ass momma can go straight to hell!" Then I pull the cover over my head and go to sleep. "Dumb muthafucka, ole momma's boy."

Chapter 3

Terri

I wake up the next morning thinking Pam was right, I don't need to be fighting. I'm too damn old. I'm so sore my arms feel like Jell-O and my legs are stiff as a board. Shit, a girl is outta shape for real. I look around and no Rome. *Good,* I'm thinking 'cause I don't feel like hearing about last night and his bullshit-ass career. So I get the phone and call my girl Rachel. She picks up on the fourth ring. "Wassup?" she asks.

"Nada," I tell her as I yawn.

"I heard about last night. Is it true you beat some girl ass at Club Luv and the ambulance had to come take her to the hospital?"

"Where did you hear that from?" I ask with concern in my voice as I sit up in my bed.

"Girl, the *Washington Post.* They say her nose was broken."

"What?! I broke her nose?"

"Bitch, I guess you did. That's what's in the paper. Girl, you ain't know?" Ra asks.

"Hell naw, read it to me."

"It reads: Last night the girlfriend of basketball superstar Rome McKnight beat young Monica Burros almost to death at Club Luv. McKnight and Burros were having drinks and enjoying themselves when Terri Morgan walked up to the couple. Terri asked Burros to leave and when she didn't, Morgan got upset and lunged over the table and started beating on her. She broke 23-year-old Burro's nose and fled the scene on foot, sources tell us. We tried to contact Mr. McKnight for his comments but we got no answer. Sources also say McKnight's girlfriend busted him in the head with an expensive bottle of champagne. We just hope he's able to play in tonight's game. We did, however, catch up with Ms. Burros who said it was just a misunderstanding and she's not pressing charges. She adds, she just hopes she and Mr. McKnight can move past his ex's craziness."

"No that heifer didn't! Who does she think she is? I know she don't want no more," I tell my girl Ra.

"Terri, let me ask you something."

"Shoot."

"Is Rome and this girl involved or is she just a groupie?"

"Knowing Rome's ass, both. Girl he told me last night to get my shit and get out."

"What?"

"Yeah."

"But did you tell him you're pregnant?"

"Nope, I'm not about to try and hold no man down by telling him I'm pregnant. I'm too fine for that shit. Where he leaves off, another will pick up and love."

"I feel you on that. Are you going to work today?" she asks me.

"Yeah girl you know I gotta check in and make sure shit is running right. Hell, that's my money."

"Look, I hear Slim is throwing a party in the ATL."

"I think I'ma go. You wanna fly wit' me?" I ask her.

"Hell yeah he gives some good ass parties. Is he still with Vicky Fox?"

"Girl, I don't know. Sister Mag had an interview with her and she says they are, but in his interview he says they not. You know how that shit goes. One minute they on and the next they off," I tell Ra.

"Girl as fine as he is, I would be begging his ass back if I was her," Ra quips.

"Now don't get me wrong, she's fine for her age and smart, but the clock is not on her side."

"Terri, I feel you on that, but how about that Pooch Hall on the show *The Game*. Now that's a keeper," Ra tells me.

"No girl, how about that 50 cent and his song, *Have a baby by me baby and be a millionaire?* Hell he just don't know I'll have ten ashy babies by him. That's 10 million, and baby you know I'ma turkey roaster."

"You ain't never lied about that shit, and on that note I gotta go and take a long cold ass shower talking 'bout Pooch," Ra jokes.

"Wait, what time you want me to pick yo ass up Ra?"

"What time you gon' be ready? Hell I'm riding wit' you on yo jet."

"Well, you gotta point. Let's say around 10pm."

"Ok see you at ten. One," Ra says, then she hangs up the phone.

Chapter 4
Rachel

"That bitch always nagging Rome's fine ass. Hell, how can she mess that up? She lives in his big ass house, she's having his child, and he gives her anything she wants. See that's the problem with some bitches, you take their asses from the hood and they forget where the fuck they come from. Now me, if Rome was mine, he wouldn't want for a god-damn thing. I would serve him pussy, ass, titties and mouth on a gold platter. He wouldn't need a cook, I would cook breakfast, lunch, and dinner, plus I would be at every game. I mean what more could a man want? Girl, he would be so damn tired between fucking me and working, Rome's ass wouldn't have time to play wit' the boys or the girls. In the club wit' a bitch? Child please! Rome wouldn't be seeing a club all the head I would be giving him. Please! Terri thinks she's the shit. She's always calling me wit' some drama. If it ain't about her, it's about the stuff she done bought. Rachel

I just went to the mall, Rachel I just got a new ring, Rachel come check out my new whip, Rachel, Rachel, Rachel. Fuck Terri and all her shit! I mean she's my girl but, she's such a bitch. She made it, I'll give her that being a sports agent and all. Hell, I'm just a teller at a bank but I do well for myself, and Terri makes me feel like I should bow down to her happy ass. I still can't believe she beat that girl's ass like that. She needs to grow up. She knows how Rome's ass is. That nigga has been the same since forever, that's how he is. He's a hoe. I mean who hasn't had his ass? She needs to just shut up and deal with it or move on, don't you think Pam?"

"Are you done? I mean are you gonna let a sista talk? What you mean everyone had him? Did you fuck him?"

I get silent for a second. "Hell nah! How you sound? Fuck my friend's man? Where they do that at?" I tell her and I pray she believes it.

"Look, Terri is what she is, but she's been a good friend to the both of us. Let her be who the fuck she is. Feel me?" Pam comes back.

"If you say so. Anywho, are you going to Slim's party in the ATL?"

"Yeah. Me and Toni going. Who you going wit?" she asks me.

"Oh me and yo girl Terri," I told her since she says let her be who the fuck she is.

"She didn't even ask me to go, bitch!" Pam yells through the phone.

"Ole well, it is what it is. I guess you and Toni will be driving and I'll be flying. Holla," I tell her then I hang up the phone. *Take that bitch,* I say to myself smiling.

Chapter 5

Terri

So I'm walking to my closet, I open the door, "OOOOOOH...
my...God! Noooo...that bastard didn't! I'ma kill'em!"

Now my heart is racing and I'm in a frenzy. This nigga
done cut up all my shit, my mouth is twitching and I'm mad
as hell. I'm so fucking mad I don't know what to do! I start
thinking about my jewelry and I run to open my safe that
is in the wall of my walk-in closet. No the hell he didn't!
How did he get the combination? My jewels are all gone!
This fool has gone insane. He doesn't know who he's messing wit'. I'ma get his black ass! He wants drama? Oh, I'll
give him drama. I stop and think no... no... no! I know he
ain't do what I think he would do? So I run to the garage
and swing the door open. Nooooo, not my baby! Nooo...
my husband. He destroyed my baby, oh hell no my Aston
Martin Rapid I paid $209,995 for. *His ass will not get away wit'
this shit! HELL NAW!*

I go back in the house and I call my girl Boo. She answers on the first ring. "Hey girl," she says.

"Boo, I...I'm..." I can't even talk I'm so mad my mouth is foaming.

"What's wrong girl?" she asks. She knows I'm heated.

"Girl, I'm getting ready to get psychotic!" I yell in the phone.

"Calm down. What's going on?"

I'm breathing heavy. "That crazy-ass brother of yours done cut up my clothes, smashed all my windows, and slit my tires," I tell her in one breath.

"Not your Aston Martin!"

"Yes, that's the one!"

"Why not yo BMW?" she says, knowing I don't care about the beamer.

"My point exactly."

"So what you gon' do?" she asks.

"What can I do? I've got to go shopping and get new clothes and call the dealership."

"Is that all he did?"

"Hell that's enough, short of taking all a sista's jewels."

"Girl I'm on my way, give me an hour. I'ma bring you something to wear."

"Oh, no thank you. I love you and all but you can't dress."

She gets mad. "Well from what you just told me, beggars can't be choosy."

"Honey nothing about me says beg, and why did I call you anyway?" I ask her before hanging up the phone in her ear. *Guess-for-best wearing ass.*

So I call Pam and tell her my situation. "So that nigga thinks he can just treat you any kinda way?" Pam says. "I'm on my way. I'll bring you some Seven jeans, an Anne Klein sweater and some Miu Miu Booties."

"OK that'll work 'cause that damn Boo offered to bring me some..."

Pam cuts me off, "Girl, say no more." We bust out laughing and then she continues. "I'll see you, don't worry we can handle this."

I just sit on the couch rubbing my belly thinking I can't believe I'm one month pregnant by this fool. I've never seen this side of him, but if I tell him I'm pregnant then he's gon' think I'm trying to trap his ass, and I ain't no groupie. I knew when he went pro he was gon' start acting up, but I got this. I'ma lose this baby and live my life with or without his ass 'cause I got my own.

Chapter 6
Terri

"Pam, you know my ass is too big for these jeans. I'm pulling and pulling, girl I feel like I'm gon' pass out."

"Well bitch it's the best I can do. Hell you need to stop eating."

"So bitch you calling me fat?"

"If the pants of a 9-10 bitch don't fit, then yeah I'm calling yo ass fat," she tells me and we laugh. "We need to get outta here and get you some new clothes."

"I already called Gee, she's my shopper. She'll be here later to drop off a whole new wardrobe," I tell Pam.

"Must be nice," she says with her bottom lip poked out.

"Pam, don't start it. You know I'll do anything for you. Hell I bought you a house, yo Max, and clothes, plus I put money in your account every month. What more do you want from me? You, Tonya, and Ra ain't never happy."

"Oh a sista not complaining, I'm congratulating," she says with a fake smile.

"Whatever, Pam, let's go. I don't know what in the hell is taking the dealership so long to get here and pick up my husband."

Pam and me walk out the house, and the tow truck guys show up.

"What took y'all so damn long to get here?" I ask when they step out of their truck.

"We had other jobs," the fat ass white man says to me.

"I don't care. My car is the first car y'all should've came to get!" I yell at the fat dirty-hair looking fucker. So I open the garage for them to get my husband.

"Damn Ma what happened?" the young black guy asks with his fine ass, but he's broke. No play for him.

"That is not your job to be asking me what happened. You just tow the muthafucka, and take good care of him!" I yell. He just looks at me like I'm crazy. "Here are the keys, and you two better believe I'ma call the dealership and tell them you took two hours to get to me."

Pam and me stand and wait for them to put my baby on the flat bed. When they do, I call the dealership to let them know what time they got here and when they was leaving. I don't want any more problems with my car.

"So what you gon' do about a house?" Pam asks as I'm driving.

"Janice is meeting us at Paulina's so she can show me some places."

"So you really leaving his ass this time."

"Not really, but if that's what he wants to think, then yeah. Pam, I was thinking about making you my beneficiary. How do you feel about that?" She looks back at me, like I just asked her for money. "Why you looking like that?"

"'Cause I'm in shock, bitch. I think you should hold off on that. I mean you are having a baby."

"Yeah, if I don't get rid of it. And anyway you're going to be the godmother, so if something was to happen to me you would be the one taking care of it. You know Rome's ass gon' be too busy wit' the hoes. I'ma call my accountant right now and set it up. Is that ok wit' you?" I ask her.

"Well yeah, if that's what you want."

I call my accountant to set up an appointment.

Chapter 7

Rome

I come home and see she's not here. That's a good thing though. Now don't get shit twisted, I love the hell outta Terri. I mean she's smart, beautiful, she could be Meagan Good's twin sister. The best thing is she brings in her own money and that nobody can complain about. She's definitely wifey material, but a brotha is too young to get married, plus my moms don't care for her. Don't know why, but she don't. I think she wants me to have somebody that depends on me. Hell I definitely don't want them headaches. When Terri makes me mad, she makes me do shit I don't normally do. Like the shit she pulled at the club, she made me so mad I cut all her shit up and messed her car up. That was some gay-ass shit when you think about it. I'm just glad that shit didn't hit the news; it just hit the newspapers. I called Gee and told her to go and replace all her clothes and I'ma put her jewels back. I just wanted to make her feel the same damn pain I was feeling at the time. I know she ain't take my ass serious when I told her to get out.

I wonder if she watched the game today. I was getting my hoop on! Let me call my boo to see what she's doing. I dial her number.

"Hello?"

Good, she answered the phone. That means she's not too mad at a brotha. "Hey babe, it's yo boy."

"No one's my boy, remember? I got 30—oh my bad, 29—days to get out."

"Look, you miss me or what?" I ask.

"Miss you, why would I miss you? You ain't go nowhere."

"You got jokes. Did you watch my game?"

"Why would I do that? Ask one of your stank hoes did they watch yo game."

"Look man, where you at, and when you coming home?" I ask her, trying not to pay her no mind 'cause I know she's playing games.

"Nunya, and don't be asking me no questions. You lost that right when that groupie slipped and fell on your dick."

"So you gon' play games all day? You know a nigga love you girl, na'mean?"

"Rome, that ghetto shit ain't gon' fly this time. As a matter of fact, go tell yo fat ass momma that shit. Maybe she'll give you some!"

"Terri see that wasn't necessary, was it?"

"Yeah it was since she told yo ass not to be wit' me."

"See Terri you always bringing up the past."

"Rome, don't you know the past affects the future."

"So what you saying?" I ask her.

"This..." *Click!*

"Terri, Terri..." I can't believe she just hung up on me. She must be mad as hell, she's never missed any of my games. Maybe I went too far wit' the car, but she bust me in my head and I had to get 12 stitches, but she don't see that though. Man fuck this I'ma call Karen.

"Hello?" Karen answers.

"Hey Karen, wassup?"

"Nada."

"Can a nigga come through?"

"Can a bitch come through?" she says back.

"Now you know my situation."

"Yeah, and when you gon' handle that situation?" she asks.

"Oh very soon, as a matter of fact, sooner than you think. She's moving as we speak."

"I would hope so since she bust you in your head at the club."

"Girl that was a misunderstanding."

"Yeah, if you say so."

"Look, I'll be over there in 45. Make sure my shit is tight before poppa gets there."

"Whatever, nigga. See you in 45."

Now that's what a nigga needs, some love. So I take a shower get dressed and head to Karen's. As I drive down I-95 my celly rings. It's my man Byron.

"Hey man what you doing tonight since we off tomorrow?" he asks me.

"Headed for some juice," I tell him.

"For some juice, nigga? Yo shit gon' fall off," he jokes.

"That'a be the way to go, don't ya think?" I joke back.

"Man Slim's having a party in the ATL, you trying to fly out wit' us?"

"That'a work, but let me call Karen. I know her ass wanna go."

"You talking about phat Karen wit' the big bodacious ass and the E size tits and shit?"

"Yep, that's the Karen."

"Man that chick got a body that'a make a 90-year-old man's dick get hard."

"That's my boo," I tell him

"But what about Terri?"

"Man she's *histo*."

"Nigga, that's what you say."

"No, I *know* nigga."

"Nigga you crazy. Terri got the brains, looks, and she's sexy. Man she could be Meagan Good's twin, without makeup!"

"Yeah I'm feeling you on that, but sometimes you outgrow people, feel me?"

"Nigga how do you outgrow a woman making millions and sexy?"

"Nigga when she bust yo ass in the head," I inform him.

"Yeah nigga she must'a juggled something."

"Look man we going or not? I ain't got time to be sitting here talking to you 'bout my bitch."

"Hell you just said she wasn't yo bitch no mo."

"Funny," I tell him.

"Man meet us at Dulles Airport in about 2 hours."

"That'a work. That'a give a nigga like me some time to get a little."

"Man I think you playing wit' that girl's life, 'cause if Terri finds out she is gon' die."

"Man let me handle that. One," I tell my man Byron and end the call.

Chapter 8
Terri

"Girl this party is dope! Slim sho know how to give a party!" Ra says.

"And you know this! All the celebs are here! But don't you embarrass me in here being a groupie," I tell her.

"Girl, I've been around you long enough to know the number one and two rules. Don't stare and don't ask."

"You've got it," I tell her with a fake ass smile.

"Girl look. Terence J, he is so fine oh my goodness!"

"Where girl?" I ask her with excitement in my voice.

"Terri, there goes Pooch Hall!" Ra says as she points to the bar.

I look over that way 'cause I love me some Pooch Hall. "Girl that ain't no Pooch Hall. That's Rome's ass!" I shout with disappointment.

"Oh I don't have my glasses on. Anyway if that's Rome's ass, then he's a fine muther when he cleans up."

"What is his ass doing here anyway?" I whisper to her as I see his ass wit' a girl on his arm giving dap to his boys like he's the man.

"Girl fuck'em. Look over there, Diego Cash and Collios Pennie! Shit, you don't need Rome 'cause all the big boys in the house tonight," she tells me, trying to get my mind off Rome and the bitch he's wit. "Terri, who is this party for anyway?"

"Nobody, he's just having a party. Look there goes... Zack Miller. I've been wanting to catch up wit' him. He's going to make a bitch a lotta money if he signs wit' me. I'ma go talk to him. I'll check you in a minute," I tell Ra before heading over to talk to Zack.

As I'm talking to Zack I look over and see Pam's ass talking to DJ Faze. She didn't even tell me she was coming. Let me find out. So I give Zack my card and get his number. He tells me he wants to sign wit' my company. Now that makes an up and coming bitch like me feel extra.

I turn to go over to where Pam is, 'cause Rachel's ass done disappeared on me. As I turn to walk away, "Bingo," I whisper to myself. No other than the NFL star Byron Hall! He's gon' be my excuse to go over to the bar where my man is. So of course I make a detour and prance my happy ass right over. "Hey B," I say, greeting Byron.

"What's up, Terri?" Byron asks as he raises outta his seat to give my sexy ass a hug. Now you know I'm looking fly. Hair fly, makeup flawless and I'm Gucci down from jewels to clothes and this bitch that Rome's wit' is a Guess hoe. So I look in Rome's direction, giving him the eye. I got a few things I wanna say, and you know he's looking like a pale ghost right about now. He didn't think I would be here. But I play it cool. I don't wanna look like I'm begging and shit 'cause fly bitches don't beg, right?

Chapter 9

Pam

"What's your name, cutie?"

"Who me?" I ask.

"Well since there's no one else around us, yeah I would be talking to you."

"Oh, Pam Tracey Booker. And what's your name?" I say to him real fast. A bitch is pressed.

"Faze," he responds.

"*The* DJ Faze?" I play it off like I don't know who the hell he is, but you know damn well I do.

"Well is there another DJ Faze?" he asks, looking at me funny.

"No, not that I know of," I tell him, feeling like a small roach.

"You're not a blond for real, are you?" he asks me. Then I look at him and we both bust our laughing. "Can we sit down and talk?" he asks.

Hell, what happened to a brotha asking a sista if she wanna hydrate her mouth and shit. But 'cause I don't see another option, I say, "Yes, why not."

Faze and me sit down and shoot the shit for about 20 minutes, then I see Rachel coming my way. One thing you must know about this bitch, she's a muthafucking gold digger and a playa hater.

"Hey boo," she says to me, then she gives me an air kiss on both sides of my cheeks.

"Hey back to you," I tell her wit' a fake-ass grin.

"So who is your friend?"

"This is DJ Faze. Faze, this is Rachel."

"Well hello Mr. Faze. Look, when you ready for bigger toys come see a sista," she whispers to him. I can't believe this bitch. I wanna choke her ass. But instead I choke on my drink.

"I'll pass," he says to her. "The lady I'm sitting with is all good with me. Don't you think?" Then he looks into my watery eyes from choking on my drink.

So I look at Rachel. "Now was that necessary?"

"What? Girl, I was just playing. You ain't take me serious, did you Faze?" she asks him.

"I'm glad to hear that you wouldn't do your friend like that. I'ma go over here and let you girls talk," Faze says as he gets outta his seat and walks away. But before leaving, he gives Ra his card and tells her to give him a call. You know I was heated but I couldn't show it.

"Ra, you are such a bitch. Talking about Terri on the phone today. Rachel, she's nothing like you," I tell her.

"I know," she says walking off with her head held high.

"I'ma get yo ass one day," I whisper to myself as I take another sip of my XO, looking over at Terri, who looks like she's up to nothing good at the bar talking to Rome and some girl.

Chapter 10

Terri

As I stand at the bar looking good as hell Byron asks me, "What you doing here, Terri?"

I answer him in a loud voice so Rome and his hoe can hear me. "I'm here on business. Zack is going to sign with T&M."

"Hell you getting ready to make a lot of loot. He's the hottest thing in the NBA right now."

"I know Byron, that's why I'm signing him. Only the best for the best," I tell him. Then Rome sucks his teeth. Now it's my opportunity. "So, hi Karen," I greet.

"Oh, hi Terri. What you doing here?" she asks with a dry voice.

This hoe gon' stand in my face with my man and act like she ain't hear my convo with Byron, but that's ok I got something for her ghetto ass tonight. "Well you know I'm a busy woman that's busy making money, I mean. What you doing here?" I ask her as she moves closer to Rome, rubbing on his arm now.

"Rome wanted me to keep him company tonight." Trying to talk like she's a baby.

"Oh you two a hot item now? Not that you wasn't before," I spit.

"Terri don't start no shit," Rome interrupts.

"I'm cool since I got 28 days now. Hell it's 12 midnight, correction 27 and I wasn't talking to you anyway. Karen is a big girl. It takes a big girl to play with the big boys," I tell him while rolling my eyes at the bastard.

"So Karen, my question?" I ask again wanting her to answer.

"Terri I ain't got time for you and yo insecurities, so step the fuck off!"

"Excuse me I didn't know I stepped on. Did I hit a nerve? Karen, you don't have to worry about me, you can have Rome's sorry ass," I assure her.

She puts her hands on her hips and says, "Baby, I been having Rome—me and everybody else."

"Karen, if everyone else been having Rome then why would you want'em? That lets me know you have very low self-esteem and you just right down whorish. But I do agree with you. See, since I've dumped Rome, he's turned to trash. Speaking of which, aren't you gon' be late for your IHOP job? You're still the manager, aren't you?"

"Terri..." Rome buts in.

"Rome, you don't have to defend me. She's just mad 'cause she has c-cups and that no-ass-at-all disease. See when you wit' me, you can get the full package," she says, rubbing on her tits and ass.

"Karen, I make five million a year and you make…let's say 25,000 a year give or take, so who has the full package? Tulu," I say then turn to walk away.

"No, I have the whole package 'cause I got yo man. Ha, ha, ha!" she spits laughing out loud.

No that bitch didn't. And she was so right, my stomach just fell. I was so mad but wasn't shit I could do. So I turn around, look at Rome and go into actress mode. I lift my hand and rub my belly while walking away. "Bye-bye, baby daddy." If you could see the look on this nigga's face, his lip drops and he moves away from that bitch so fast you would've thought she had a disease. I hated using my baby like that but a bitch gotta do what a bitch gotta do.

Chapter 11
Terri

I walk over to Pam. "Hey Pam what you doing here?"

"Well no thanks to you, I drove up with Toni."

"You did? Where she at?"

"Somewhere, I don't know," Pam tells me with an attitude, but I pay her no mind.

"Can you believe Rome?" I ask her with my arms crossed.

She turns and looks at me, rolling her eyes upward. "Aw yeah that ain't nothing new and I thought you was done with him," she snaps.

"Well excuse me, what they put in yo drink?"

"Nothing. I'm just tired of you and Rome's shit. Either you gon' be wit' the nigga or leave his sorry ass."

"Now hold up Pam, only I can call his ass sorry, not you or no one else. Anyway, what was you and Faze talking about?"

"Nothing, he wasn't feeling my ass, he gave Rachel his card."

"Oh well, dust yourself off and try again," I tell her. Then I look over at Rome's ass one last time, only to see him kissing and hugging on that bitch in my face then looking over at me out of the corner of his eye. That's ok, I got something for that. I reach in my Gucci bag and pull out two 80mg Oxy's. See I keep this shit for the haters. It's better than a gun. I walk up to the bar and order one Ice Tea 'cause she looks like an Ice Tea kinda bitch. As the bartender goes to ring me up I put the already crushed pills in the drink and stir it up. When the bartender returns, I ask him to give the drink to the lovely lady standing with Mr. McKnight. "No problem," he says as I hand him a $20 tip. The bitch musta asked him who was it from, 'cause he pointed over at me. So I quickly hold my drink in the air, calling a truce. The dumb bitch took the bait. She puts the drink to her mouth and downs it all.

Yes! was all I could think.

I walk back over to Pam. "Girl, let's not waste the night being mad. Let's party." I grab her by the arm and we hit the dance floor. We were on the dance floor for about 30 minutes and all of a sudden we hear all this chaos. We run to the noise and we see Karen on the floor, people are standing all around her. One man is giving her mouth-to-mouth resuscitation. However, the mouth-to-mouth did not work.

The bitch is dead.

I look at Pam and tell her, "I'm getting ready to go. Did you see Rachel?"

I am so calm at this point, but Rome damn sure ain't. Wait until this hit the fucking news. I think, *Wanna fuck wit' me, do you?*

Pam looks at me all suspicious. "Terri, did you have anything to do with this?" she whispers while holding on to my arm.

I look at her real serious like, "Girl, you know I ain't no killer. I was partying wit' you." She lets my arm go and I start looking around for Rachel, so we can get ghost.

Chapter 12
Rome

"Man, I can't believe this shit keep happening to me," I tell my man Byron.

"Yeah man that was some crazy shit last night. I wonder what made ole girl fall out. I mean she was talking one minute and the next she just fell out and died."

"I know. After she got drunk, she passed out. Maybe the drinking was too much for her," I tell my childhood friend.

"Man the bad thing is, I didn't even get to hit before she tapped out," I add.

"Now man, that there is some sick shit. That girl just died and all you can think about is the juice. Rome, you got some unresolved issues," he spits while we play *NBA Live* on the PlayStation.

"So what you gon' do about Terri? I mean she did say baby daddy, and I ain't never known her to play wit' no shit like that," Byron says while whooping my ass. He's got 58 points to my 26 and I'm the NBA star.

"Man I haven't given it a second thought. Since what happened to that girl, shits been all over the news media blowing up my agent's phone and shit."

"You gon' answer it?" he asks.

"That's a dumb question," I tell him. "Hell naw. What I look like boo-boo the fool?" Then my cell rings. I look down at the caller ID. "But I'ma answer this one though," I tell him. "Hello?"

"Hey babe what you doing now?" the girl on the other end asks me in a sexy voice.

"Why?" I ask.

"Because I'm horny, and your daughter misses you."

"Where you at?"

"Home, you coming or what?"

"You know I am. Ay … what was you doing at the party last night and how you get there?" I ask her.

"Pam wanted to go, so I drove up so I could be wit' you but I see you had your hands tied."

"I told you I didn't want you hanging around Pam. That bitch is a hoe."

"Rome you can't tell me what to do until you put a ring on this finger."

"C'mon girl you know that wasn't nothin' at the club, and that ring is coming real soon. I'll be there in about 2 hours."

I tell her all this to keep her from telling Terri about our daughter.

"Ok whatever you say. You wanna talk to Peaches?"

"Naw I'ma see Shorty when I get there. I picked her up some Jordan's and some clothes. Did my accountant send you that money this month?"

"Yeah."

"So you good then?"

"Rome." She calls my name softly.

"Yeah?"

"When you gon' tell Terri about Peaches?"

"Let me worry 'bout that, you just have them panties off when a nigga get there."

"You so nasty," she tells me.

"And guess who likes it?"

"Funny," she comes back.

"See you in 2," I tell her then end the call.

"Man, Terri gon' kill yo ass when she finds out about Peaches," Bryan chimes in.

"She's good. Terri ain't going nowhere. And if she's pregnant like she say she is, I'ma make her wifey. That's all she wants."

"What?! Man now I know you done lost it. She'll be sure to find out about little Peaches and kill you and the mother. As a matter of fact let me ask you now, do you know what color you want your coffin nigga, while you play-ing?" Bryan says.

"Oh well, I'll cross that when it comes. Look nigga I'm out," I tell my man while pulling 5G's outta my pocket to pay up for the ass whooping he just gave me.

"Do come again nigga, it was a pleasure," that nigga tells me while smelling my money and smiling. Bitch ass nigga.

Chapter 13
Rachel

I've been trying to call this nigga all day, no answer. Now I know I blew T-Ray's dick some'em fierce like, so why he ain't answering a sista's calls? Oh well I did get a stack outta his ass while he was sleep. Hell maybe he found out. Who knows? All I know is I been wit' T's ass for 12 years and 2 babies and he still will not marry a sista. I love his dirty undies so damn much. Well, as long as he ain't bringing nothing to the house he ain't take out, I'm good.

Let me stop and get this dirty car washed. It ain't been washed since Jesus was a baby. Oh my God, is that Papa?

Honk! Honk! I honk my horn to get his attention. "Ay, Papa!" I yell.

"Yo what's up Ra?"

Now Papa is one fine ghetto ass nigga and the nigga is paid. So I drive up to him and get out my car looking like I just stepped outta hoochie mamma heaven.

"Damnnnnn...ummmm. You looking fine as hell," he tells me while licking his full lips.

"You don't look bad yourself. Where you been?"

"I've been around," he says.

"You getting yo car washed?" I ask him.

"Nah, I'm getting the windows darker."

"Why? So nobody can see yo black ass when you getting head nigga?"

"Is that what you trying to give a nigga?" he asks me while looking around and holding his crotch.

"It depends on what you working wit."

"Damn, Ra, you always on some money shit."

"Hell yeah, a bitch gotta eat too. How about two stacks nigga?"

"How's about a stack?"

"A stack?" I ask with my lip turned up.

"Ra, your head must be gold talking 'bout two stacks."

"No nigga, it's double platinum," I tell him then he chuckles.

"Ok, meet me in the bathroom."

"The bathroom?"

"You got a better place?" he throws back.

"A'ight," I agree, then I get my fruit cocktail—that's my little secret—and put it in my hand bag. Then I go into the shop's bathroom. "Ok ... Papa, money first."

"Damn, girl," he says while rubbing his chin.

"Don't girl me. Pay up first," I tell him, holding out my hand.

He digs in his pocket and pulls out a wad of cash. "See, if you was my girl you could have all this."

"Papa, I ain't gon' lie, you got all the right ingredients but they also point to baby mamma drama and hustler bunnies, and my ass ain't got time for neither, feel me?"

"Girl, I ain't got no baby mamma."

"You say."

"Here," he says, handing me the money.

I count it while he's standing there showing his gold grills. Them gold teeth look so good.

"Alright it's all there, one thousand strong," he tells me while pulling down his pants. I pull out the fruit cocktail and put it in my mouth. I chew and then start sucking his dick so good, this nigga bust within 10 strokes. Then he says, "Ra, I want some more of that. Damn girl that's some powerful shit you got and what's that shit in yo mouth?"

"Oh my little secret and sucking you off again is no problem, but that'a be another stack."

"What?!"

"Yo ass heard me," I tell him, holding out my hand.

"Look bitch, you gon' suck my dick!" he says through clenched teeth and holding his raw big-ass dick.

"Whatever, nigga. You want some more, you gotta pay," I tell him, looking up still on my knees.

I get up to walk out the sticky ass bathroom. Papa grabs me by my weave. "Bitch!" he shouts.

This muthafucka is crazy. I know my head ain't that damn good. A bitch ain't doing nothing for free. "Nigga, you betta get the fuck off me," I tell him scared as hell. My heart is racing 100 miles per hour.

"Fuck that! You gon' get yo hoe ass back on them knees and suck my dick! Then when you done, you gon' let me stick it in that phat ass of yours."

Bow, Bow! Papa punches me in my face and then in my eye. Now I know this nigga done lost his mind if he thinks he's going in my ass after fucking my face up and that shit hurts like hell. Don't nobody enter this ass but T-Ray and T-Ray ain't never put his damn hands on me. So I go into actress mode, but I swear a sista's face is stinging.

"Ok...whatever you say."

"That's what I thought," he says.

I get on my knees, lick the head of his dick, rub on his ass, then I place my lips on his balls. You like that daddy?" I ask him with my mouth full of his balls.

"Yeah, right there," he tells me, moaning and shit.
Crunch!

"Awwwwe...ooo. Shit! You bitch I'ma kill you *awwweee!*"

I bite down as hard as I can while reaching in his pocket wit' my right hand pulling out all the cash I can grab. Then

I let go of his balls and haul ass. I'm running through the shop fast as shit.

"Ra, Ra … Ay, Ra," Berry, the owner of the shop, calls me.

I turn to him and yell, "I'll see you later." I get to the parking lot, unlock my car with the keypad and jump in. "Car start," I say. It starts up and I floor it. All you could hear was my tires screeching outta the parking lot. "Woo now that was a close call," I whisper to myself.

I'ma have to stay away from the shop for a minute though. I pull into the 711 parking lot on Livingston Road. I count the money I grabbed. *Damn it's ten stacks here, I hit the jackpot!* I back out the 711 and go home 'cause a sista had a hard-ass day. I know my face is gon' be fucked up tomorrow so I think I'll go and lay my black ass down.

Chapter 14

Boo

I park my car, grab my VC bag and go into For-U-Insurance Company.

"May I help you?" the young girl at the front desk asks.

"Yes you may, I'm here to see Tyron."

"What's your name?"

"Oh just tell him it's Boo."

"Do you have a last name, Boo?"

"Look just tell him Boo, Rome's sister."

"Ok Boo, Rome's sister, have a seat," she demands, picking up the phone to call Tyron.

He walks up to shake my hand like we ain't never had fuck relations. Ole little dick bitch-ass nigga, but I play it off 'cause I need him right now.

"Brittany McKnight," he says.

No he didn't just call my whole government.

"Tyron Davis," I spit back.

"What brings you to my office or this neck of the woods?"

"Hell ain't no woods around this ghetto-ass office, but I need an insurance policy," I tell him.

"You're in the right place for that, follow me." I follow him to this big office even though it's in the heart of south-west DC. We sit down and he continues, "Now what type of policy do you want?"

"I need a life policy, about three million dollars' worth."

"Damn that's a lotta bread, Ma. I mean, not to be rude, but how much are you worth?"

"What you mean, how much am I worth? What's that got to do with the tea in fuckin China?"

"Well the underwriters won't back an insurance policy for that amount unless you're worth at least half that amount. Meaning do you have a house, cars, jewels…what's your net worth, how much do you own or are you going to own? Is anyone leaving you anything? Stuff like that," he explains to me.

"It's not for me."

"Oh, I see. Then who may I ask is it for?"

I get up, walk around his big desk and whisper in his ear.

He responds, "In that case, no problem. But who's going to sign the paperwork? They will also want to run some tests for that amount."

"Will 20 G's get us past all that?" I ask him.

"Hell yeah! I'll start the paperwork myself." He calls his receptionist on the speaker phone. "Mrs. Harris, bring me the paperwork for a three million dollar life insurance policy."

"On my way," she responds.

"How long will it take?" I ask him.

"About three days. Call me in three days."

"I'll do one better. I'll be here in three days at one o'clock."

"Boo, I'll see you then."

Chapter 15
Terri

I'm standing in the bathroom of me and Rome's house playing wit' this nasty ass whitehead on my face. And it ain't even that time of the month, shit I'm pregnant. This muthafucka just will not go away. Shit. *Pop.* Yes, finally.

Then I hear, "Terri, Terri where you at?" No this crazy-ass nigga ain't home already. I thought I was gon' have some girl time to myself. "Terri, Terri, where you at?" he calls out again.

"I'm up here!" I yell back. I know it's gon' be drama 'cause I hear his big-ass feet pouncing up the steps.

"Terri?"

"Yeah?" I answer.

"Why you ain't tell me you was having my baby?"

"Yo baby. Nigga please. How you know it's yo baby? All them free-fuck cards you been giving out over the years."

He looks at me as he scratches his head. "Girl, you ain't busting a grape."

"Oh, you think not?" I tell him with my arms across my chest and one of my eyebrows raised.

"So is it?" he asks.

"If it is?"

"I'ma take care of mine."

"Yeah Rome it's yours. I'm not keeping it though."

He steps back. "What?! What you mean you ain't keeping it?"

"That's what I said. Rome, you fucking too many bitches. I can't keep going through this shit wit' yo ass!"

"All that's gon' stop now that you having my baby. Terri, this is all I ever wanted was a true fam."

He reaches in his pocket and pulls out a big ass rock. "Look what I got you."

I start crying. "This is all I ever wanted is to be Mrs. McKnight," I tell him, smiling from ear-to-ear, looking at the ring.

"A 10K ring," he says while placing it on my finger. "If this ain't big enough we can go back to Jacob's and he'll make you a bigger one."

"No this good. Baby it's damn good."

He gets on one knee. "Terri Morgan, will you become Terri Morgan McKnight?"

"Yes! Yes! Yes!" I'm so damn happy and stupid. I jump in his arms and we kiss and make love all night. I'm so glad I got rid of that whitehead first, though.

Chapter 16

Rome

I wake up the next morning with Terri in my arms. She looks so damn beautiful as I look her whole body over. How could I ever do her the way I've been doing. I move off the bed slowly not to wake her up. I go to the bathroom to shit, shower and shave in that order. I get dressed and head out the door. I get into my whip, pull off and call my man Berry making sure we still on for tonight. Then I call my baby mamma.

"Hey," she says.

"Hey what you doing?" I ask, trying to soften her up for the blow I'm about to deliver.

"Nothing, getting Peaches ready for daycare. Why?"

"Why you always taking her to daycare? You don't work. Why can't yo ass stay home wit' her?"

"'Cause I got shit to do," she replies.

"Like what?"

"Like going to the salon and listening to stories about her father hooping and fucking bitches."

"Oh, you got jokes."

"Whatever," she comes back.

"Anyway, I called you to let you know I'm marrying Terri."

"Oh really, and what made you want to do a thing like that? I thought you was leaving her ass. At least that's what Pam said in the shop yesterday, or she was leaving you, some'em like that," she rambles on trying to piss me off.

"First of all, Terri will never leave me. And how about I told you not to go to that hoe-ass Pam's shop. See that's why you could never be my wife, you don't listen to a word I say."

"Who said I wanted to be your wife, nigga? You's a hoe. Only Terri would put up wit' that shit you putting down. And when she finds out about Peaches, she'll be sure to leave yo ass," she tells me with a stink-ass attitude.

"Well, she won't find out about that until our baby is born."

"Y'all what?!" she yells though the phone.

"You heard me," I tell her, but I don't think she's feeling it.

"Ok Rome, whatever you say. So are you coming through tonight?"

"Girl, didn't I just tell you ... I was getting married!

I can't mess around no mo. I'm sending you your money every month and coming to see Peaches, that's it."

"We'll see," she tells me real dry like.

"Hey, if you think about calling Terri and telling her about Peaches, I'll cut you and Peaches off from all my money and I won't come to see either of you. Peaches will only have a trust fund. Do I make myself clear?"

"I hear you loud and clear, masa."

"So we a'ight?" I ask her 'cause it's nothing like a woman's scorn.

"We a'ight," she says again wit' a dry tone.

"A'ight, holla," I tell her then end the call.

Chapter 17

Terri

I wake up and the space beside me is empty. I look over at the clock on the nightstand. "Damn I was sleep forever, it's 6pm. Rome musta went to work or had an out of town game," I say to myself. I get up and call Zack. I need to get the contracts over to him and his lawyer.

"Hello?" he answers.

"Hello, may I speak to Mr. Zack Miller." I know it's him on the line, but I try to sound all professional and shit.

"This is he."

"Hey, this is Terri Morgan. Look, I would like to fax the contracts over to you. If it's ok."

"That's good, you got my fax number?"

"No, but I do have your lawyer's. Would it be ok to fax them to him?"

"That's fine with me."

"Mr. Miller, after you look them over with him, can you please get back to me, let's say around Monday of next week?"

"Will do." He pauses. Terri?"

"Yes, Zack."

"You think I can take you out one day?"

"Zack, if this relationship goes well, you can take me out every day," I tell his stupid young ass.

"Bet. Fax them to him and I'll look them over. If nothing's wrong, I'll sign them and have them back to you by Friday," he says with excitement in his voice.

"Ok, I guess I'll be talking to you then."

"For sho," he says then we end our call.

I get outta bed after taking care of business and throw on my robe. I go into the bathroom and start brushing my teeth. I hear a noise and some footsteps getting closer. I figure its Rome so I pay it no mind. Then I lift my head and look in the mirror ... "OOOOOOH...SHIT...NOOOO!" I yell.

"Don't scream, bitch!" the person behind the black mask orders me. I cover my mouth wit' my hands, my toothbrush falls on the floor. I feel all life within me pouring out as this person turns me around and stands in front of me with a gun pressing against my temple.

Then this person runs the nose of the gun down my breast, stopping at my vagina. I'm thinking please don't kill me, I'm pregnant. Then pushing me against the sink, ripping off my robe, the intruder takes the gun and places it in my vagina and fucks me with it. I want to scream from the pain

I'm feeling. It seems like it's lasting for hours. He grabs my weave and throws me on the floor, pistol-whipping me in my face. I start to feel blood flow from my head. I'm hanging in there until the last blow to my temple ... that's when I start feeling myself losing life.

Chapter 18
News Report

"We have breaking news, NBA superstar Rome McKnight's fiancée, sports agent Terri Morgan, was raped and beaten almost to death at McKnight's house in Bowie, Maryland. The police have no leads on who may have done this horrific crime. The Maryland Police are asking if you, or anyone you know, have seen anything to please contact them. McKnight is offering a cash reward of one million dollars if anyone can lead the police to the person or persons who did this. We will keep you updated on any further developments. Dan, back to you."

"Sue, that's crazy. First she breaks a bottle over McKnight's head and beats up his date, then McKnight is in Atlanta at one of Slim's parties and his date falls out and dies from God knows what. Now this. I know after all this is over, they'll want to take a long vacation."

"Well, Dan, sources tell us that Ms. Morgan is pregnant with McKnight's child."

"Woo, I hope this doesn't put a damper on his skills on the court."

"Well, we shall see. In other news, the Bullets..."

Chapter 19
Rachel

"I can't believe this shit. Did you hear that Terri got raped? Who would do that to her?" I ask my home girl Toni as we sit in her living room watching TV and eating cereal.

"You're the one always saying she's a bitch," Toni says.

"Well, that she is. I wonder if they stole any of her furs or jewelry. The big question is where in the hell was Rome at?"

"Girl, you know how that no good nigga is. He probably was in somebody's pussy."

"I hope it wasn't none of his women that did this, 'cause that nigga got a lot of them," I tell her, wanting her to know she ain't the only side piece.

"Are you going up to see her?" Toni asks me.

"She's your friend, too. You not going to see how she's doing?"

"Yeah, but not today. I gotta get Peaches ready for her little trip. The daycare is taking her to the pumpkin patch."

"Awwww ... that's cute, so you gon' play mommy today?" I ask her, being funny.

"Fuck you. I always play mommy," she responds with attitude.

"You need to go and find her a daddy," I tease.

"Now why would I have to do that? She already has one," she tells me with her mouth full.

"Well I ain't never seen one. Where is he?"

"Just 'cause I don't put all my business out there, don't mean he ain't there for us."

"Don't get all mad, I was just playing."

"I ain't mad, I'm just telling you how it is. I know women, you bring yo man around them and they got their nails out ready to scratch."

"I know you ain't talking. I see how you be looking at Rome and you never miss none of his games."

"Child please, that's because Terri is my best friend and through her I've grown to love Rome as well."

"Ok best friend, if you say so. I guess that's why pumpkin patch is more important than yo besty, you know the one who just got raped? On that note I gotta get to the hospital to see my real best friend. Oh, Toni?" I call her, so she can look at me. I want her to see I'm being real and she can't play games wit' me.

"Yeah." She looks away from the TV at me.

"Please don't call me yo best friend. 'Cause if you think I don't know Rome is Peach's father, then you got another thing coming. See I really love Terri, so I would never tell her what I know. You always saying Rome some shit. Well start smelling yourself! I'm out," I tell her leaving her mouth wide open as I put my empty bowl down, grab my bag off the table and walk my happy-go-lucky ass out the front door. "Fake bitch," I whisper to myself as I wait for the elevator.

Chapter 20
Rome

"Man, I can't believe this! My life is spiraling out of control. My girl is in the hospital and all they can worry about is whether I'ma be able to play. B, if I was home, this shit wouldn't happen," I tell my main man Byron."

"Look man, it isn't on you. How would you know this shit was gon' happen and you had a game to play?"

"Yeah but still, I feel so damn bad she's in there fighting for her life and our baby's. It ain't shit I can do man," I tell him as I break down and cry. "B-man, I can't lose her or the baby. I don't know what I'll do without Terri. I love her man I do."

Byron pats me on my shoulders and assures me, "It's gon' be alright. Man you think it was one of your shorties?"

I put my hands on my face. "Man, that's all I've been thinking about," I confess.

"Well we need to focus on getting her outta here then, we'll work on the rest."

"Man when I find out who did this to her in my fucking house, I'ma dead they ass!"

"I feel you man, I feel you," is all he can say.

"Hello, Mr. McKnight," the doctor greets as he walks in the waiting room and shakes my hand.

"Hi Sir, what's going on wit' Terri?" I ask him with my eyes still full of water.

"Ms. Morgan had some bleeding in her brain. We managed to stop the bleeding, however she does have some hairline fractures within her face. She's suffered some swelling in her vagina area as well. In time it will go down. Now, I must warn you she looks worse off than she really is. In time all her wounds will heal. Ms. Morgan is a strong lady. Mr. McKnight, as far as the baby, he's going to be just fine," the doctor tells me.

"Hey! Did you say he?" I ask with excitement.

"Yes, Mr. McKnight you and Ms. Morgan are having a boy."

"Yeah that's what a nigga talking 'bout!" I yell while jumping up and down in the waiting room. People are looking at me like I'm a nut. "When can I see her?" I ask the doctor.

"You two can go in now, but I must warn you she's heavily medicated and she has tubes in her mouth and nose.

"Ok thanks doc, you don't now know how much this means to me, you saving my girl and our baby," I tell him and head back to see my future wife.

I walk in her room and a tear falls down my face. "She looks like she's dead," I tell B. We walk over to her and I kiss her tenderly on her forehead. She blinks and it looks like she is smiling. "Terri, I hope you can hear me. I never knew how much I cared about you until now. Now if you can hear me, know I love you and I'ma find out who did this. And when I do, he or she is a dead man."

"Yeah, Terri, I love you. Pull through and hang in there," my man Byron tells her standing on the other side of the bed.

"Baby, I'ma go now. I got a game, but I'll be back in the morning. Oh yeah, it's a boy, Terri! I planted a male seed in you. Baby thanks for being my boo," I tell her, then kiss her on the cheek and we bounce.

Chapter 21
Rachel

"Rachel."

I hear my name being called while I'm getting my shop on. So I turn around and it's no other than Boo, Rome's sister.

"Hey Boo," I greet with a fake-ass grin 'cause for real, I don't like the loud-mouth hoe.

"Hey Ra, what you been up to? I ain't seen yo ass since Jaws was a fish." She looks me up and down, with her hand on her hip like I got shit on me.

"I've been around. Where you been?" I ask her.

"At the hospital spending time wit' Terri," she tells me like I give a damn. But I did ask.

"Yeah I go up from 6am to 10am," I tell her.

"Oh I didn't know that. Rome didn't tell me," she says, looking stupid.

"Did she come to, yet?" I ask her.

"Not as of yesterday."

"Shit it's been three days now! I have a feeling she'll come to soon," I try to assure her.

"Have Pam and Toni been up to see her yet?" she stands in front of me and asks.

"Hell girl I'm not my sista's keeper. That's some'em you gotta ask them."

"I feel you on that. I'm sorry to hear about you and T-Ray. I mean I knew Pam is a fucked up person but to fuck T-Ray and get pregnant! Bitch now that's a bit much," she tells me without blinking an eye.

Now you could buy my red ass for a dollar as I'm standing here speechless. This bitch thinks she's got one on me, but I'm too smart for that.

"Oh my God I'm sorry. You didn't know!" she says as she covers her mouth.

Now this messy bitch needs her diaper changed. How she gon' ask me about Pam a minute ago, then say the shit she just said outta her mouth. She knew I didn't know but it's ok, I'll play along with her ass. "No, it's not that I didn't know. I just didn't know that anyone else knew."

"Oh well that's a good thing, I thought I let the cat outta the bag. And what did you do to Papa 'cause that bitch-ass nigga been asking about you all around the 'hood."

"Fuck Papa! That nigga thought he could rape me and get away wit' it, but I showed his ass!" I tell her.

"What?! Papa raped you? Oh my God all the bitches he get, why would he do that?" she asks me with disgust written all over her face.

"I don't know. Why don't you go and ask his ass. I'm shopping," I tell her and take my clothes to the checkout counter.

"See ya!" she yells to me as I'm walking away.

I pay that rat-ass bitch no mind and walk on. "Hater," I whisper to myself. I can't wait to get to Pam's ass. I would fuck T-Ray's ass up too, but his ass is overseas doing a show. Fucking rappers always got they dick in somebody's pussy.

Chapter 22

Pam

I'm in my salon curling my client Tonya's hair, and guess who walks in, Magic's ass. "What's up, Magic?" I say to her.

"Nothing. Was up wit' y'all?" she spits.

"Nothing at all girl. I'm just trying to make a dollar outta 15 cents," I tell her, trying to make convo.

"Yeah I know how that goes, but you shouldn't be having money problems."

"Child please who don't?" I come back wit.

"I hear you and T-Ray kicking it. That's why you should be good in the pocket anyways."

"Where in the hell you hear that shit at?! T-Ray and me, who told you that lie? Whoever told you that has lost they damn mind! 'T' is my girl's man. Why would I be fucking him?"

"Well you need to tell him that. 'Cause he told G-Man you and him was fucking and your pussy is tight, and your head game is crucial."

I stop curling my client's hair who is all ears about now. "Are you sure he said Pam Thompson?" I ask her, holding the curlers in my hand. Damn I wanna hit her in her big-ass mouth with them.

"For sho', and it ain't no mo' Pam Thompsons around here but yo ass," she says while pointing at me and sitting her ass in my waiting room.

"Ronny's not here today, so who you want to do your hair?" I ask her, hoping she would walk her ass outta my shop.

"I want Perry's gay ass to do my hair then."

"Ok he's almost done, he'll be right wit' ya," I tell her keeping the gossip down.

"I'm sure," she says while crossing her legs and picking up a magazine to read.

Now why did T-Ray tell G-man that shit? He knows Magic fucks with him and her mouth is loud as all outdoors. Let me call his ass. So I'm pulling my cell out my cape, when Magic calls my name again.

"Pam."

"Yeah," I answer her.

"What's up wit' yo' girl Terri? Is she gon' make it? I mean you been to see her?"

"Yeah I've been to see her, and yes she's gon' make it, but I may need to give her a makeover."

"Her face that bad?" she asks like she's really concerned.

"Somewhat."

"What's her room number?" Perry's gay ass turns and asks me, being messy.

"I can't remember," I tell him, rolling my eyes.

"Ummm ... I bet you can't. Girl, I'm glad I only work for yo ass 'cause with friends like you, I damn sho don't need enemies."

"Perry whatever, you don't know where I've been."

"Wit' T-Ray," Magic blurts.

"Fuck both y'all," I tell them. Then I tell my client I'll be right back. I go in my office so no one can hear me and call G-man's fat black ass.

"Hello, who dis?" G-man answers.

"It's me fat boy, Pam."

"Yo what up?"

"You fatty, why you putting my business out there like that?"

"What business? You got me fucked up, baby girl."

"No you got me fucked up," I spit. "Look G, I don't know what yo skilo is, hell maybe you still mad about the abortion thing who knows? And to tell you the truth I really don't fuckin' care. Yo ass was broke and you was wit' Magic. Who knew that shit would happen after fucking you two times with a condom? I mean really, yo fat ass should have told me the condom came off."

"Pam check this, I don't give a flying ass bout what you talking 'bout or your trifling-ass life. What we did, we did. That shit was over before it got started…feel me?"

"It's funny you feel that way 'cause you sho was blowing my cell up just two days ago," I remind his black fat ass.

"Grant it, my dick was hard and it wasn't no hoes on front street at the time, so I checked my memory rolodex for some fast free pussy and you came up first. I pulled your file and gave you a holla. Baby girl you know—and all the niggas on the block know—you ain't wifey material."

"Oh, whatever nigga, I gets mine and if I want to husband your black fat little-dick ass, you'll go, you bitch-ass nigga. Just keep my name out yo fuckin mouth."

Click.

I don't believe this fat bitch. He's getting a few coins and thinks he's on top of shit. He still a broke ass bitch-ass nigga. He thinks he's Biggie Smalls, and the last name stands for small ass dick! Pissing me the fuck off in the middle of the day. What nigga gossips about another man's dick? Let me answer that…*A Bitch-Ass Nigga, that's who!*

So I call my folks …

"Look, I need you to handle something for me…"

Chapter 23
Terri

I open my eyes. Thank God, I think I'm still alive. I think I heard Rome's voice, or was I dreaming? I adjust my eyes to the bright light shining in my face. Ok I'm alive. I feel my face, I feel tubes coming from my nose and mouth, then I realize I'm in the hospital.

"Welcome back, Ms. Morgan. You gave us quite a scare," this nurse is telling me as she looks at the machines that surround me. I try and talk but I realize I can't because of this stupid tube in my mouth. I signal her for a pen and pad with my hand.

"You want to say something?" she asks me.

I nod my head "Yes." She reaches in her white jacket and pulls out what I need to communicate.

What happened? I write.

"You were attacked," she responds.

Attacked! By who? I write.

"Now that, my dear, is for the police to worry about. You just need to rest."

Did Rome and Pam come to see me? I'm curious.

"I don't know a Pam, but Mr. McKnight has been here every day since your accident. He's been sleeping in that chair right over there. As a matter of fact, he just left this morning. He has an out-of-town game today. I think he said Chicago. Would you like me to turn the TV on so you can watch his game?" she asks me in one breath.

Yes. I write.

She goes and turns the TV on, then she returns. "Is there anything else I can help you with?" she asks.

Yes, what about my baby? I write as my eyes start to water.

"For now the baby is just fine!" she says with excitement.

"I turn the paper over and write, *When am I going home?*

"Well you've been asleep for three days. The doctor will be in tomorrow morning. I'm going to call him to see if I can take your tubes out so you can be a little more comfortable. If that's ok with you?"

Sounds good to me! What hospital is this?

"You're in Johns Hopkins, you were in Prince George County Hospital, but Mr. McKnight had you moved here."

Has anyone else come to see me?

"Let me see. The football player, Byron, Tonya, your mother and father are in town and I think your sister Rachel, is that her name?"

Thank you, I write, feeling defeated and disappointed 'cause no one else had come to see if I was ok, like my so-called friend.

"Oh, there was a Boo-boo that came as well," she turns around to tell me. I just nodded my head. "Well Missy if you need me, I'll be right outside your door. I'm all yours for eight hours, then Mrs. Smith will be in. Mr. McKnight hired us personally, so we are all yours. Hit this red button if you need anything ok?" she tells me.

Ok, I write as she shoots something in my I.V. then I black out.

Chapter 24
Rachel

"I'm so fucking pissed right now, I don't know what to do. Where is a parking space? Shit, fuck it, I'ma park right in front this raggedy ass place. I'ma go up in here and beat the brakes off this fake hoe-ass bitch!"

I walk up in Turning Heads Beauty Salon. I'm walking fast so I know this bitch sees I'm mad.

"Hey, Ra," Toni speaks while sitting in Pam's chair getting her doo done.

"What's up, Toni?" I respond with my hand on my hip.

"Nothin'," she says. She continues to try small talk 'cause she can see something isn't right. I dismiss her convo and approach Pam's ass.

"Now Pam how long you been fucking my man?" I ask her, rolling my head and eyes reaching over top Toni's head, pointing my finger in Pam's face.

"What?! I ain't fucking no T-Ray!" she shouts back.

"Well that ain't what I'm hearing in the streets, bitch!"

"Fuck what you hearing in the streets. I'm standing here in yo face telling you I ain't fucking no T-Ray! Don't he live in the ATL now? So how would him and me be fucking? I think you need to tell yo CI to stop smoking crack!" she's yelling. So I know she's guilty as hell cause she's trying to throw my ass off wit' that ATL shit.

So I step around the chair and start pointing closer in her face. It's getting ready to be on up in here. "I know you fuckin'em 'cause he told G-man about yo sorry ass head game!"

"First off, ain't nuttin' sorry about my head game and second T-Ray ain't yo fucking juice no mo, and third..."

"OK y'all stop. Both y'all my girls and I ain't gone see y'all fight over no nigga," Toni jumps between us and says.

I look at Toni. "Bitch yo ass just as stupid, you been fuckin Rome's ass forever," I tell Toni, putting her on blast street as spit flies out my mouth. Then I look at Pam, with my arms across my chest. "Hoe!" I call out.

"Yo Momma a hoe!" she yells.

That's it, I think to myself. I pick up the Marcel hot curlers...*Boop!*—one to the head. She picks up the stove and throws it at me. "You muthafucka!" I yell as the stove hits me in my head. I jump on her short ass, pushing her against her hair station. *Boom!*—right. *Boom!*—left. I'm punching her in her face. All I hear is get off her, get off her, as somebody is pulling on my hair. I turn around and start swinging.

Crack! in my face was all I felt as I hit the ground. Pam gets a punch in. That bitch is strong as hell! I knew that going in though. I knew I was gon' have to get the first lick. I'm on the ground and she's kicking me in my face. This bitch is beating the holy shit outta me.

Ronny finally gets her off me. "Bitch get the fuck outta my shop, and don't you ever bring yo nasty ball-biting ass back!"

So I'm on my feet now with Ronny holding me up, and Toni holding Pam's Pit Bull ass back. "Ra, you ok?" Toni asks with concern in her voice.

As I start to walk out the shop, I can feel blood running down my nose. I turn around and look at Toni. "No I'm not," I tell her as I walk through the doors to go to my car. My feelings are crushed. I thought Pam was my girl and shit.

Toni comes outside with me. "Why would you come up in this girl's shop acting like a fool? You know Pam is sweet with her hands." Toni sounds all innocent and shit. She makes me sick too.

"That's a'ight, Toni. I'ma get her ass," I tell her while breathing heavy 'cause my fat ass is outta breath.

"Look, just let it go," she says. "She's not wit' T-Ray, and if she was, he ain't worth all this."

"Now it ain't about T-Ray," I tell her.

"C'mon Ra, it..."

Pam cut's her off. "Let that nasty bitch go and c'mon so I can finish yo hair. As for you bitch, come in my shop playing bad again. I want you to know you can see me anytime, you always gon' get the same results. Know that!"

"The nerve of this bitch! She fucks my man and she's having his baby. So tell me how she gon' be mad at me?" I ask Toni.

"Don't worry, I'll talk to her, it's gon' work itself out. It always does. You gon' be ok," Toni says before going back in the shop.

"Yeah," I tell her with a napkin over my nose and my hair all over my head. I just wanna cry. I lost one of my so-called friends and my man in one day. When I get in my car and look in my mirror I can't believe it. I look like a chickenhead and the worst of it is Pam is my stylist. I gotta give it to her, she's the best in D.C., but it's ok. TW is working at Giavonnies Day Spa and Salon, and he is just as good.

Fuck Pam! Payback is a bitch, I tell myself as I speed off.

Chapter 25

Rome

"Hey baby girl."

"Hey yourself."

"So you gon' let me in or what?"

"I opened the door, didn't I?" my sidekick says and walks away leaving the door wide open.

Damn her ass is so fuckin phat! I think to myself. "You looking good as always," I tell her.

"Whatever, you want something to eat?" she asks.

"You," I tease while grabbing her 24-inch waist. This girl is phat to death. She's dark skin, dark brown eyes, long black hair, pretty white teeth, triple D breasts and an ass like Buffy The Body. Her ass is so phat and she's self-made—nothing fake. Plus she makes her own money. Not as much as Terri, but she does good for herself. The best thing is she has no strings attached. *I love it,* is all I can think to myself.

"Boy that's all you ever wanna do. Here, take the remote, I'll be right back," she tells me as she goes to her room.

I sit down and start to watch some sports highlights when I turn my head to the right, "Dammmmmn...Baby Damn! You sho know how to get a nigga there."

She's looking sexy as ever with her black thigh-high high heel boots. I love me some thigh-high boots on my women. She also has on a black leather mask and a black leather cat suit with a long whip in tow.

"Damn...cat woman!" I shout. My dick just grew ten inches.

She turns on some Jadakiss, then she turns around, gets on her knees and makes her ass cheeks jump one by one. She is facing me now, she's taking the hot candle wax and pouring it on her long wet tongue. *Shit*, I think, *I'ma bust right now.*

After all that, she does a fuckin split and cracks the whip.

I jump 'cause a nigga ain't into that whip shit. I'll leave that shit to the white boys. But she still looks good doing it.

"Take all yo shit off," she whispers.

A nigga like me do what he is told when it comes to some good ass. She crawls over to me with her tongue out, taking a cube of ice out of my cup that's on the coffee table. She places it in her mouth with a peppermint. After that, she places my dick in her mouth and starts sucking it real slow like.

"Yeah baby suck it, suck it baby real good. Right there yes...damn baby yes. That ice feels so good my dick feels the breeze," I moan, rolling my eyes upward with my toes curled in between the carpet.

She is really getting into it now. She starts sucking and slobbering all over my dick. Her slobber is running down my balls. I grab her hair and pull on it, pushing my dick in her mouth deeper as she starts to speed up. I catch her rhythm and start fucking the shit outta her mouth. She stops me and takes my dick out. *Damn what she do that for?* I ask myself.

"Rape me, Rome. Rape me," she orders.

I smack her on her face and start ripping her shirt off. Her breasts fall out. I grab them and put them in my mouth, biting and squeezing them one after the other while she is jerking on my dick. I push her on the floor and plunge my big black dick in her juicy ass pussy.

"Yes, Rome, yes fuck me pleazzz...fuck me. Don't stop...faster you nasty *mutha-fucka*, faster I say!"

"Fuck baby *woooo*...this some good ass shit, baby damn you gon' make a nigga cum too quick!"

"No don't, don't cum yet. Put that dick in my ass, Rome. Do it, just do it!"

I pull my dick out of her warm ass pussy. Shit, I hate doing that. Then I ease it in her asshole.

"Woo…Woo…fuck me daddy big dick, fuck me!" she's yelling.

I place my right hand around her little neck and my left hand over her mouth. I dip in and out of her asshole. My dick is getting harder and harder. In and out, in and out, she's moaning muffled noises.

As I long-stroke her, I'm looking at her chocolate ass bounce back and forth. I remove my hand and grab the pillow on the couch, not missing a beat. I turn her over and place the pillow over her mouth, causing her to lose her breath, then I put her legs around my shoulders and penetrate her asshole once again, but deep this time.

She is trying to yell, moving her head from side to side. "Rome, Rome…oh my goodness Rome, please fuck it, fuck it, give it all to me, yes!" she screams as the pillow falls from her face. So I choke the shit outta her with both hands. The vein in her neck pops up and she turns red. I continue to bang the shit out of her ass.

"Baby, I'm…I'm shit baby shit *Awwwww* Shi...fuck!" I yell at the top of my lungs. Then I bust all in her. I slow down and take my dick out slowly. While she is still on her back, I place my face in between her sexy legs and suck all the cum out her pussy. She hisses. I run my tongue up her body to her full sexy brown lips. Our tongues meet and caress. I slip my dick back in her and it's on all night until six in the morning.

When I get up to leave, I look over at her sleeping with an ice pack on her pussy. Damn, when she do that? I musta been knocked out and didn't even know it. A nigga is slipping. I start thinking back to my shorty, Terri, who is laying in the hospital…shit Terri ain't got nothing on me and my baby's sex life, but Terri got her when it comes to business. Why can't I have this pussy and Terri's brain? Well I guess that's why they say you can't have the best of both worlds.

"Well, off to pick up my wife to be."

Chapter 26
Terri

"Hey, Baby," my fine ass man says as he enters the hospital room to pick me up.

"Hey yourself. What took you so long?" I ask him.

"I had to stop by the gym to pick up some stuff for tonight's game."

"Oh, I missed you so much last night. I tossed and turned all night. I can't wait to get home in my own bed."

"And I can't wait to get you home. What the doc say about you know what?" he whispers, raising his eyebrow looking at my kat.

"Boy that's all you think about," I joke

"Well I'm all man, what you expect?" he replies.

"Have you heard from Pam? It's not like her not to visit me or show up to see me."

"Baby I told you them hoes ain't yo friends, they just cornballs. They wanna be you, but you can't see that."

"Ok, we not gon' go there today. Today is my day to shine," I tell him.

The nurse walks in the room. "Ms. Morgan, are you ready to go?" she asks me.

"Hell yeah!"

"Well you have to wait for Mr. Patterson to get here with the wheelchair," she informs me.

"Wheelchair! Oh hell nah, I can walk!" I tell her with my eyes wide open.

"It's up to you," she says.

"C'mon baby just let her do her job," Rome says in a low tone of voice.

So I shoot him a look. "Ok if you say so. Are we going anywhere before we go home?"

"No, why you wanna go somewhere?" he asks me.

"Well yeah I would like to stop past the shop to see Pam. I'm a little worried about her. I'm telling you, this ain't like her."

"Why you worried about that hoe? I hear she fucked yo girl Rachel up."

"What! Why? Why would she do that?"

"Something about Pam fucked T-Ray."

"Pam fucked T-Ray? Why would she do some shit like that? If she did, why would Ra fight her over T-Ray? I mean he's a hoe," I tell him, then I thought about how I would have reacted and left it alone. "I know, don't even answer that," I order Rome.

"Well here is the wheelchair man. It's time to go," Rome says as he swings the wheelchair around for me to get in. "You still want to go past Pam's shop?"

"No, I don't feel like all that drama," I tell him, and we exit the room.

Chapter 27
G-Man

"Hey man, wussup?" I ask my man Jerry as I walk into his shop.

"You, nigga. You trying to do that or what? Man you know about that green?"

"It's whatever wit' me nigga," I respond.

"I feel you, I feel you. This how it's going down. My man Will is gon' drive the car, me and you gon' go in the bank and act like we sticking up my girl and she gon' walk me to the vault and boom—$300,000, feel me?"

"Oh yeah I'm feeling that. A nigga feeling that on the real, you heard."

"I hear, I hear clear."

"Now get this…no blood. This is an easy in and out situation, know what I'm saying?" Jerry tells me like I'm stupid.

"I got you man, so when this poppin off?

"Now, my man is in the car, you rolling?"

"You ain't said nothing but a word."

We go to the car that is waiting for us outside. As I get in the back, Jerry introduces me to his man. We ride out and reach the bank. We put our masks on and get out of the car with our guns in tow. We enter the bank, pass two tellers working and go into his girl's office. He puts the gun to her head and walks to the vault while I stand in the lobby.

"Don't nobody move, get the fuck on the floor!" I yell. My palms are all sweaty and my heart is racing.

After about what seems like forever, this black-ass nigga returns with two duffle bags on his shoulder and no girl. He fires two shots in the air. "Listen up, take off all y'all clothes and lay back on the floor face down, don't nobody move. If anyone moves or tries to call the popo when I leave, then I'ma find you and kill you, so give all your IDs. After you count to 100, then you can get up."

The customers in the lobby and the two tellers do what they are told.

Then Jerry looks at me. "You good?"

I nod yes.

"Let's ride then," he utters. Then we exit the bank through the side door where his man is waiting. We hop in and his man pulls off but my heart is still racing. We take our masks off as we ride down the street. I look out my window and see the cops flying down the other side of the street towards the bank. *I guess they didn't count to a hundred,* I think to myself.

"Man that was sweet, 300 G's. We did it, we did the damn thing," he yells with excitement.

"The world is mines *WooWoo*! Shit now that's what I'm talkin 'bout. Take what's yours!" his man yells as he pulls into the garage.

"G-man?"

"Yeah," I answer while bending over, taking off my boots.

"Thanks man, but this the end for you nigga," he tells me with his cold steel pressed against the back of my head. I knew it was over but I don't understand why.

"Man c'mon, man you can have it all, man just don't do this, not like this…"

Pow!

I fall and …

Chapter 28
Terri

We get to our new house in Fort Washington, Maryland. Rome moved because he didn't feel safe at our old home since all this happened.

"Rome, this is beautiful. And we right on the water-front! This is so nice. Did my parents call you today or did they go back to New York?" I ask him as we pull up in the driveway.

"No they didn't call. I guess they'll call later," he says as he puts the truck in park.

As I was about to get out the truck, Tonya and Boo surprise me by opening my door. "Hey girl, welcome to yo new bad ass house!" Boo says with a big smile. "Yeah girl, this place is the bomb, c'mon now! I'm so happy yo ass is home. We made you something to eat!" Tonya adds with excitement.

"Maybe I should go to the hospital often if I can get this kind of treatment, and who cooked? If you cooked Tonya, then I just might be going back sooner than my checkup time," I tell her, joking.

"So you got jokes. Whatever you say, c'mon let's get you in the house," she tells me while the both of them take me by my arm and help me up the steps to the door.

Rome is getting the bags and balloons out of the back of the truck. "I'll be in, in a minute babe," Rome yells as we walk away.

I look back at him. "Ok, baby," I tell my handsome ass man.

Tonya turns the knob to the front door of the house and we walk in. "Why is it so dark?" I'm asking ...

"Surprise!" my welcome-home guests cheer.

"Oh my God! Y'all got me good Tonya I'ma kill you and Boo!" I spit. I'm overwhelmed, so my baby-ass starts to cry.

"C'mon," Byron says as he hugs me. Then Rome's ass comes from nowhere hating, knowing Byron's got all the right ingredients to make a girl say yes to leaving any man she has; nevertheless, I'm wit' his best friend Rome. Byron and me decided we was not gon' have sex anymore. Damn my pussy was mad about that shit. Anyhow, Rome interrupts, so I look at Byron and mime "thank you" wit' my lips. People are hugging and kissing on me. I'm feeling so blessed right now. Tonya starts the music and they start partying. I'm a little tired so I sit down on the couch and Rome sits by me. "Rome," I whisper to him.

"Yeah, babe?"

"Where is Pam, baby?"

"I didn't invite her."

"Why?" I ask.

"Terri, I don't think she's yo fucking friend, she's too sneaky. She's a hoe."

"What makes you say that?" I ask him.

"Look baby, can you trust yo man and let it go?" he says to me looking me dead in my eyes.

So I call my girl Tonya over when Rome gets up and goes up the steps. She comes over to me. "What's up you having fun?" she asks me.

"Oh yeah, lots of fun. Can you bring me my cell so I can make a call?"

"Yeah sure girl." She goes and retrieves my cell phone. I dial Pam's number. She answers.

"Hey Pam what you doing?" I ask her.

"Hey baby girl where you at?" she asks.

"I'm at home. Rome threw me a party and you're not here so I want you to come over."

"Well I'm kinda in the middle of some...Oh forget it, I'll be there."

"I'll have to give you the new address. You got a pen?" I ask her.

"I didn't know you moved."

"Yeah I didn't either."

"Ok, I'm ready. What's the new address?"

I give her the address and we hang up the phone.

"Who was you talking to?" Rome asks me.

"That was Pam."

"She called you?" he asks with attitude.

"No," I tell him, then get up and go to the kitchen to get some water.

Chapter 29
Byron

I see Terri sitting by herself moving her head to the music, so I go and take a seat beside my old good friend. "How you holding up?" I ask with my arm around her shoulders.

"I'm holding up. I look worse than I feel. This situation just made me realize how blessed I am to have good friends in my corner. It just feels good to see you all having fun under one roof, my true friends," she looks me in my eyes and tells me.

"You are so right, friends are a blessing. But you know it's just little ole me. I'm saying you can be 100 with me. I'm going to ask you again, how you holding up…I mean with everything in your life?"

The smile leaves her face. "Byron, I don't know why someone would wanna kill me. Yeah I've done some foul shit in my life, hell I'm still doing shit but nothing that no one don't deserve. And as far as Rome, I know men gon'

be men, y'all gon' be hoes and shit. I remember when you and me was a hot item. You left me to go back to your baby momma, and that's ok. You thought you was doing the right thing. I just could never understand why you didn't tell me about her when we got together. Why you never told me she was two months pregnant before my feelings got involved? See, that's what men do. With Rome, I don't have to worry about baby momma shit. At least I know if he's fucking around, he's wrapping it up. He may be a lot of things, but disrespectful he's not. Shit when I think about it, after all we went through, you and Nana ain't together anymore. Now ain't that a muthaucka? She left you for a movie star. What goes around comes around. I guess that's why I'm in this position today." She has water in her beautiful eyes.

I clear my throat, thinking to myself, *If she only knew.*

"Word, word but Terri do you know your self-worth? You're beautiful, smart, funny, fun and let us not forget *rich*. Oh yeah, and self-made. What more can a person want or ask for? Yeah I fucked up and I feel it every time I see you and my boy together. Terri, I never told you this, but I love you now and I loved you then. A brotha just scared of a powerful woman such as yourself. I know with a hood rat, I could control everything and you're right, Nana got stronger, opened her own business and met a star and rolled out on me. But get this, I didn't care 'cause it was you I loved, not her."

"Thanks. I just wish you would have told me this a long time ago. Now it's too late."

"Is it?"

"Now B, you know I love Rome and he is your boy. I'ma file this convo and move on. Being rich and beautiful doesn't mean I don't have feelings and it don't mean I won't fall in stupid love like now. As you can see, this is my problem. I don't know how to get out of this and I don't know how much more I can take before losing it. Yeah me, Terri, the big self-made millionaire know-it-all. She can't control her own damn life when it comes to men. And get this, I may be rich as hell but it's one thing money can't buy and that's tomorrow. Byron, I can't buy the next day or hour, so I'm gon' sit here and enjoy the minutes I am having with my good true friends. Feel me?"

I take my finger and wipe her tear, then I give her a soft kiss on her forehead for the food for thought she just gave me. "Terri, you can always count on me. I'm here for you. Whatever you need, I'm here. But I need you to keep your eyes and ears open."

"I am. I just wish you could knock some sense into your boy's head."

"Oh believe me, I tried more than you know."

"Thanks, Byron, for being here for me and thanks for being a good friend to me and Rome."

The thing is, I don't think Rome is a friend to her. It seems to me he's just using her to get what he wants—built-in sex, I think to myself as I get up to go get another beer.

Chapter 30

One Hour Later
Rome

"Byron man, Pam looking phat as a snicker in them jeans. Damn a nigga's dick is hard. I'ma have to hit that before the night is over, know what I mean?"

"Man she is phat but I still say you playing wit' fire, and my momma always told me when you play wit' fire you always get burnt," my boy tells me.

"I feel you on that shit, but it seems like she's getting phatter and phatter by the day. Her ass is bigger than J. Lo's."

"Now boy that's a big ass, any ass that's bigger than J. Lo's!" a voice shouts from behind me.

"My main man Berry. When the hell you get here?"

"Man I heard you was having a get together with a lot of ladies, so I thought I would just stop through."

"I feel you man, I can't wait for Terri to fall asleep. Feel me?" I tell both of them with a chuckle.

"Boy you out there," Berry tells me as he takes a sip of his beer.

"That's why they call me Red Dog," I say and we laugh, giving each other dap. Pam turns around. She musta felt us looking at her. Our eyes lock. I signal her to go upstairs and she nods her head in agreement. "Well man y'all enjoy the food and ladies. I'ma go pay the water bill, I'll be right back," I tell them.

"I bet you will nigga," Byron says, looking all curious.

"What you doing here?" I ask Pam.

"What you mean, I can't come to my best friend's house party?"

"Bitch stop calling her yo best friend. You wouldn't know how to have a best friend if they handed you everything you wanted on a gold platter."

"Why I gotta be a bitch, Rome?" Pam asks me.

"My bad, hoe. Is that better?"

"I don't see you complaining when you fucking this hoe, nigga."

"Girl stop gumming me and get my dick up," I tell her.

"Pull it out, nigga."

This girl turns me on so much. So I unzip my pants and pull big Kong out. Pam gets on her knees and starts sucking my Johnson.

"Yes, *uuum*, suck it girl," I tell her while pulling her hair, moving her head back and forth with force.

"You like that, daddy?" she asks me with her mouth full.

"Hell yeah, don't stop bitch, suck daddy off," I demand. She starts sucking faster and harder. "Pam, Pam, baby you gon' make a nigga nut in yo mouth."

"Don't nut, fuck me first," she says as she takes my dick outta her mouth and stands up, pulling her jeans off. All of her phat round ass pops out like a Jack-in-the-Box. She bends over, spreading her dark chocolate ass cheeks apart. "Put it in Rome, fuck me. My pussy is so hot and wet, it needs you daddy," she moans.

I love it when she talks dirty. I slide my dick in her pink ripe pussy.

"OOOOOOH... yeah fuck me Rome, *pleazzz.*"

I'm blowing her back out, fucking the dog shit outta her. "Touch them toes," I order her. She does just that. I'm fucking her so hard her head is hitting the bathtub.

"I ... I'm cumming, Rome!" she yells out loud.

"Shush, girl, they might hear you."

"But I can't help it, this big black dick is so damn good. Ooh ... nooo. I'm cumming, baby, shit it feels so good!" she starts yelling.

She squirts white thick cum all over my dick. I love it when she squirts! After she cums, I pull my dick outta her pussy and plunge it in her asshole.

"*Awww shit, Rome,* that hurts so bad but feels so damn good. Fuck it harder, harder!" she yells.

After about 20 strokes, I utter, "Pam, *wooooo...* girl, here it comes. Take it baby, damn yo ass is so tight. Shit girl take daddy's dick, all of it," I tell her as I bust nut all in her ass. My legs are so weak. I pull my hard dick out of her as she turns around and looks at my dick.

"Boy you still hard, you want some more?" she asks.

"You know I do," I reply. But you know I want some of them full wet sexy lips. So she gets back on her knees this time, playing with her tits and takes my dick in like a pro, sucking on my balls and running the tip of her tongue up my shaft, sucking the head of my dick then making it touch the back of her hot-ass throat.

After about 10 minute of this good sucking I yell, "Pam!"

"Yes daddy cum for me."

"Take this cum." When I say these words she starts sucking fast and hard. It feels so good my asshole is tingling. "Shit, I'm getting ready ... shit, *Pammm!*" I yell. As I nut in her mouth she looks up at me and gargles my nut in her mouth, then she swallows it all.

"Rome, your nut taste *sooooo* ... Oh shit," she whispers, raising up with my dick in her hand like she just saw a ghost.

Chapter 31
Toni

"You's a nasty bitch! I should've known yo ass was fucking her. She ain't nothing but a hoe and yo dirty, nasty, no-good-ass…fucking her raw at that! How could you do this and you in Terri's house? That poor girl ain't been outta the hospital for one day… forget it Rome, it's over! I'm done. I'm tired. I don't even know what I see or saw in yo bitch-ass anyway. As for you Pam, how could you do this to us, to Terri?" I ask with my finger in her face. I know the bitch didn't wanna try me. Rome is just standing by the sink looking dumbfounded.

"Bitch, I know you not talking. You have a baby by Rome! You been fucking him forever, don't hate 'cause I'm getting mines too. Or are you mad cause you not fucking him right now? Always remember this, it ain't fun if your homie can't get none. Share and share alike, Bitch!" the bitch yells while pointing to her nasty pussy.

"Pam, you's a sick-ass bitch. All you doing this for is money!" I tell her now all up in her grill.

"Bitch, I got mines and hell yeah, Rome is adding to it. See I'm not stupid, I know this man will never leave Terri, but you on the other hand ..."

"Stop... y'all both need to chill out. Pam, get dressed and meet me downstairs. Toni, you stay right here," Rome demands with his dick still hanging. He is standing between both of us.

Fuck I love this nigga's 20-day-old draws, I'll do anything for him but right now I gotta show him he can't be doing this shit to me.

"Rome, I'm done. I mean it," I tell him.

"Shut the fuck up!" he orders, as Pam exits the bathroom eyeing me up and down.

"You wanna do some'em?" I ask Pam's bitch ass.

"Girl you ain't worth it," she replies, putting her hand in the air waving me off.

"That's what I thought 'cause I'm not Rachel."

"Fuck you and Rachel!" she spits.

Rome closes the door, then turns to me. "Look, Toni, you not my wife or my girl, so stay in yo lane. And if you think about fucking up my home..."

I put up my hand, cutting this nigga off. "Nigga, you ain't gotta worry about me fucking up yo shit. You doing a good job of that yo'self. So fuck you and yo home!" I yell loudly, not caring who hears me. I'm pissed and I want him to feel my pain.

"Bitch!" he calls me as he steps closer to me grabbing my neck, ripping my shirt and my underwear off. He turns me around, pushing me against the wall and sticks his dick in my wet hot ready pussy.

"Um, *sssss,* yes! Rome, fuck it, fuck this pussy."

"This what you want, ain't it bitch?" he says softly as he bangs the shit outta my pussy." *Smack!* He smacks me on my ass and palms my ass in his manly hands as he's thrusting in and out my puss. "Make me nut, Toni. C'mon throw that phat ass on me," he whispers.

I do just that. I start throwing my ass back on his big ass 10-inch dick. *Damn, he can fuck! That's what it is, this damn dick,* I'm thinking to myself as he continues to serve me.

"I'm cumming, *Rommmmme...*! SHIT!"

"I know, I feel you, this warm juicy pussy," he says while licking and biting on my back. "Here I cum! Toni, fuck! This pussy is so good, girl shit *ooooowww,* damn Toni fuck!" he yells as he cums in my pussy. He's breathing hard as he slows down, then he takes his dick out, walks over to the shower, turns it on and gets in. I fix my clothes, grab a rag off the towel rack, wipe my pussy and walk out the bathroom like nothing happened, like I didn't see him and Pam, like a fool I allowed him to treat me any kinda way. I guess that's why they say "A fool in love." If he didn't have so much money and some good dick, I would have left a long time ago. I should be ashamed of myself, but money over everything and that he has and gives freely. *Who knows, maybe one day I'll be Mrs. McKnight.* I'm thinking as I walk down the steps to join the others in the living room.

"Peaches, Peaches where are you?" I call out.

"Oh she's fine," says Terri. "I love her, she needs to come over more often. Maybe I'll take her to the park next week. I used to get her all the time, but here lately I've been so busy with the business. I haven't been a good godmother, have I? My little Peaches with yo cute self, you must look like your daddy?" Terri jokes as she's cooing at my baby and pinching her cheeks as she sits on Terri's lap.

"You're a good godmother, Terri, and I know she loves you too," I respond as Rome's nut runs outta my pussy down my leg.

Chapter 32
Rachel

I'm laying in bed and I hear keys in my front door, so I get up and run in the living room.

Smack!

"What the fuck is wrong wit' yo ass?!" T-Ray asks me after I smack the shit outta him.

"What you mean what's wrong, nigga?! Why! Why! Why, you have to fuck her. My best friend! Damn, what was you thinking? I've been slaving wit' yo kids, I don't ask you for nothing, Ray, shit how you gon' do us like this? On top of all this shit, she's pregnant wit' yo' baby! How and why— is what the hell I wanna know, you muthafucka!"

"First of all, calm yo ass down, and if you smack me ever again, I'ma kill yo crazy delusional ass!" he shouts, pointing his finger in my face. I see he's not playing so I move out his 6'2", 250lb way and take a seat at the dining room table.

"Now what the fuck you talking 'bout Ra?!"

"So you gon' play stupid?"

"Ra I fucked her, I make love to you."

"Nigga this ain't *Baby Boy*. This is real. Do you know how I feel right now?!" I ask him with tears running down my face.

"Yeah the same damn way I've been feeling for a while now. You think I don't know huh, do you?!" he asks with aggression in his voice.

"Know what?!" I ask.

He walks closer to me and looks down in my eyes in disgust.

"Bitch, you's a hoe. You fucked Papa for money, not just one time ... but hell I can't even count! These niggas in the streets talk Ra, damn. And don't think I don't know about Rome. Yeah, don't look all stupid now that the cat is outta the bag. Bitch, I been knowing you was fucking that cat. I just let you do you 'cause I'ma do me!" he spit.

"Rome nigga please, I ain't fucking no Rome!" I tell him, then he unbuckles his belt and drops his pants. He grabs me by my neck and chokes the living shit outta me, cutting my breathing off. Then he rips my night gown off, lifts me up out of the chair, throws me on the dining room floor and turns me around.

"Nooo ... nooo, stop *pleazz*. I'm sorry!" I cry out 'cause he starts beating me with the belt.

"This is for all the niggas you fucked, you hoe-ass bitch!" he yells, continuing to beat my ass.

When he finally stops, he grabs the back of my neck, starts chocking me again and sticks his 7-inch dick in my wet pussy. "Ummm…" I moan.

He's banging the shit outta me! He might have a small dick but he knows how to use it.

"You know why I fuck her?" he asks.

"Noooo … *sssshhh* … " I whisper, trying to answer. His dick is so good at this point I don't even care.

"'Cause you fucking the same nigga she's having a little bambino by. See baby she's not holding my seed, it's his seed she's holding. I just water it," he tells me, stroking faster and faster.

"Uh …Uh … Uh!" I'm moaning louder and louder as he lets my neck go finally.

"Shit, I'm bustin'. Shit, Ra this pussy so fucking good!" he says as he releases his nut all in me. "See, Ra, I could never marry a hoe," he says while shaking his leftover cum on my ass. "Now I'm going to bed," this fucker finishes telling me and walks away.

I love this bastard so much. Why do I allow him to do this to me? And what is he talking about, how is Pam's baby the same man I'm fucking? Fuck it. I get up and take a shower, still feeling that good ass dick I just got and climb in my bed next to my man. He climbs on me and it's round two! I love it when he beats my ass and then fucks me.

Chapter 33
Terri

Me and Boo are sitting in her living room watching *Madea Goes To Jail*. "Madea is somethin' girl," Boo lets out as we both laugh like crazy.

"I know right, she just can't stay outta trouble," I spit, still laughing my ass off.

"What y'all laughing at?" Boo's man Wink walks in and says.

"Madea, we watching her go to jail," Boo tells him.

"That joint is funny, ain't it?" Wink says.

"Sho is," I tell him, still laughing.

"Baby my lunch ready? 'Cause I gotta get back to work."

"It's on the table in the kitchen beside your blunt. It's all ready for you to do your thing."

"Good. A nigga needs some smoke right about now," he tells her, then heads to the kitchen. Me and Boo continue to watch the movie, then all of the sudden I hear ... *click, click... click*. I turn and look at Boo. My eyes grow large and my mouth is wide open. I stand and cover my mouth as piss runs down my legs.

Boo stands up and takes a hold of my face. "Terri, Terri, what's wrong?" she whispers with concern in her voice.

"It...that...it was him," I motion to Wink with my eyes.

"It was who...what are you talking about? Wink? What did he do?"

"Wink...Wi...Win...Wink...the lighter click, click... clicky. He was the one. He tried to kill me. He raped me! The lighter, that sound! I remember that sound. I will never forget that sound," I tell her with fear and hurt in my heart. Me and Wink grew up and went to school together. I can't believe he would do that to me. I start thinking and turn and look his way. His back is turned as he sits at the kitchen table, smiling and listening to music with his headphones on.

"Ok...ok," Boo says as she retrieves her cell from the coffee table. "Hello, this is an emergency. My boyfriend tried to kill my friend. Hurry, he will be leaving here soon. My address is..." She gives the 911 operator her address and hangs up.

"Terri, look at me, they will be here in a minute. You have to tell them what you know. Now c'mon, let's get you out of these clothes."

She takes me by my hand and walks me into the kid's room. She grabs some of her clothes out of her son's closet and I put them on. We are doing all this and Wink still don't know what's going on.

There is a knock at the door shortly after I get dressed. Boo looks out the window, then turns and looks at me. "They're here. I'ma go answer the door."

She answers the door and does all the talking with the police by his car while Wink stands in the doorway. I'm standing with another officer by his car at the end of Boo's driveway.

"Are you Mr. Crossford?" a male officer walks over to Wink and asks.

"Yeah, why?"

"I'ma have to ask you to turn around," the officer orders while taking his handcuffs off the side of his belt. Wink does what he is told.

"What in the fuck is going on? Boo, what you tell them? Look, call a lawyer for me please? Terri, you got to help me. What in the fuck is going on?"

Boo walks up to the car. "You bastard! You tried to kill Terri. You raped her, you bastard, I hate you!" she yells, then hog spits in his face.

151

"But Boo, Terri, Boo, I…I, Terri, wait man? I ain't, I'm innocent. What the fuck y'all do? What?!" he yells.

"Sir, watch your head!" the officer says as Wink lowers his body into the car.

"Tell the judge, you bitch-ass nigga," Boo hisses, mad as hell.

The look on his face says he didn't know what was going on, but my memory says he did it. I will just never forget that sound.

"Ma'am, do you remember the detective on your case?" one of the officers asks me.

"Yes, I do. I'll call him now."

"Please, and we will inform him we have a suspect in custody."

They leave and Boo is still crying.

"Boo I'm sorry, I'm sorry," I tell her.

"No, it's not you. You don't have to apologize. That no-good fucka deserves it. How could he? What was his motive? I hope they lock his black ass up and throw away the fuckin key."

"How you gon' make it? Are you gon' make it?" I ask her.

"Girl, I'll be fine. When Wink father died last year, he left him an insurance policy of 2 million. If anything happen to him, meaning he gets locked up or dies, then our son gets it. The thing is, we have to wait until January of next year, which is only three months away."

"At least you all will be good I will help you until then."

"Terri, you don't have to do that. My brother will give me some money, but thank you though."

"I'ma go home. I'll call you later. I need to call this detective," I tell her.

"Ok, Terri, I love you and I'm sorry."

"Don't be. I love you too."

Chapter 34
Terri

A month has passed. I've been traveling wit' Rome, and a sista is tired. I'm so happy basketball season is over. I can't wait to get things back to normal. At least I picked up 10 new clients in the interim, and no attempts on my life. We get back home. I pull my wallet out and happen to look at my license ... shit, it expires today.

"Rome, I'm going down to Motor Vehicles to get my license renewed," I yell up the steps to him.

"Hold up, I'll go wit' you," he says.

"No, I got this." I seize my Jacobs bag and leave through the side entrance, get in my car and off to the MVA. I really need a break from him. We've been together the whole season.

I get there and of course it's a long line. I'm standing in line to get my ticket to stand in another fucking line. This shit is wack. I feel someone looking at me so I look over and sho nuff this ghetto-looking, slummy looking chick wit' braids and a hoochie momma dress is looking at me.

"Hi," I greet.

"Hi," she says with bubble gum in her mouth, so fuckin ghetto.

I move up in line, look out the corner of my eye and see she's still watching me. So I say, "Excuse me?"

"Yeah?" she says.

"Do I have something on me?"

"What?"

"You keep looking at me."

"Child, pleazz. I'm looking past you. What I wanna look at you for? I ain't on no pussy!"

So I look over and see this fine ass dude wit' dreads. He has on a white T and blue jeans wit' some butter Tims and a long diamond chain. He has all the elements of a hustler. I get my number and sit down.

The hustler sits down beside me. "Can a brotha get to know a sista?" he asks.

"I'm taken," I tell him.

"I didn't ask you if you was taken. All I ask was can I know your name."

I look his cute ass over. "Terri. My name is Terri."

"That's better. I'm Wee," he informs me. Then I get quiet. "Can I take you out, Terri?

"I just told you I'm taken." Now I know he can see this big ass rock on my ring finger.

"There you go again. That wasn't my question."

"But that's my answer. See that girl over there looking at us?" I motion wit' my eyes.

"Yeah."

"Well, she's digging you. She's been watching you the whole time we been in here."

"Not a nigga's type. But you on the other hand is," he says smoothly.

He has the sexiest full lips. "Wee, don't get me wrong, you looking good. You have all the components a girl like me would like, however wit' yo ... let's say...*elements*, comes what we call hustler bunnies and I ain't got time for the hoppers, feel me?"

He looks at me and smiles. "Now I have heard it all."

"Number 54," the lady calls over the loud speaker.

"That's me," I tell him. I get up and strut a little harder than usual 'cause I know he's looking. I get my license renewed which only took, it seems...line, after line, after line. I exit the building, get in my car, start it up and grab my seatbelt to strap it in. I look down to put my car in drive. "Oh my God! Blood! What the hell?!" I open my door and step out my car. Blood starts to pour down my legs. I scream, "Heeeelp! Somebody pleazzz help me!" I grab ahold of my pants.

Wee runs over to me. "Ma, what's wrong?" I look down and he follows my gaze. "Oh shit Ma you ok? This could happen to any female, I mean shit happens," he tells me.

"No, I'm pregnant!" I scream with my hands shaking.

"Oh snap!" he says as he pulls his cell off his hip and dials 911. "It's a female here at the Landover MVA. She's pregnant and bleeding. We standing by a blue Benz and a green Land Rover truck. I'ma stay on the line until the EMT gets here."

He's holding my bloody hand. "Terri, look at me. I'm in this wit' you, I need you to hold on. Emergency medical is on the way. Sit right here, people are watching." I'm seated in my car. He is hanging in there wit' me.

"Do you want me to call somebody else for you?"

I nod my head yes. He tells the 911 operator to hold on and clicks to his other line.

"What's the number, baby?" I'm hesitant to give him Rome's number, but I need my man. No substitutes.

I tell him the number and he dials.

"Hello! My name is Wee, I have a Terri at the MVA. She's bleeding. Yeah, I called the EMT's. They're on the way... No, from her…you know…down there."

I could hear Rome yell, *"Noooo!"* through Wee's phone.

"Man, you a'ight…? You can meet us at PG hospital. I'm sure that's where they will take her…Ok, I will see you there." Then Wee ends the call. I see the ambulance coming.

Wee waves them down, they park and start taking my vitals. One of the men covers me wit' a blanket, grabs my stuff, locks my door, and helps me into the wagon.

We get to Prince George Hospital and they push me to the back. A lady asks me for my insurance info as they roll me in the wheel chair. You know they want their money! A nurse asks me what happened. I inform her, then she tells me to undress. They tell me to get on the bed, then they put an IV in my arm and push me to the O.R. I pass out.

When I wake up, I see Wee beside my bed. "Hi, shorty," he says with a smile.

I'm looking around for Rome. I feel groggy. "Where's Rome?" I moan.

"The basketball player? He said to tell you he had to catch a plane. Something about a car commercial."

"Oh, that was nice of you to wait," I tell him.

"No problem. I ain't have shit else to do," he assures me. He looks so familiar, but I can't place his face. "You want some water, Ma," he asks.

"No, thank you." I start regurgitating. He holds his hand under my mouth. "Hughhhhh!" I'm vomiting, and it runs through his hands. I'm so embarrassed. He goes to the bathroom and washes his hands, then he comes back wit' a towel and wipes my mouth.

"Sorry," I tell him.

"I'm used to it. I took care of my moms for three years. She had cancer," he tells me while rubbing my head with a cold rag.

"Sorry to hear that."

"It's ok, she's dead."

"Oh my, I'm really sorry."

"Don't be, she wasn't yo mom. So do you need anything?" he asks.

"No. Thank you anyway, you've done enough."

The doctor comes in pulling the curtain back and walks over to me, grabbing my chart that's at the bottom of my bed. "Hello Ms. Morgan. I'm Dr. Smith. How are you feeling right now?" he asks me.

"I'm a little groggy but other than that, I guess I'm fine," I respond.

"Ms. Morgan…" he begins to talk, but Wee cuts him off.

"Huh, maybe I should leave."

"No…stay with me. I need someone just in case things get too heavy for me," I tell him.

"Ok, if you insist," he says.

"Doctor, I'm listening," I say.

"Little lady, you had a miscarriage. We have given you a DNC to clean you out. Do you understand what a DNC is?"

"Yes, I do. So I lost my child?" I ask.

"I'm afraid so. However, you're young and you will be able to have many children. We also are running tests to make sure there wasn't anything specific that caused this to happen. However, I must tell you it will take the results about one week to come back from the lab," he states, looking at both Wee and myself.

"Thank you sir for everything," I tell him, holding back my tears. *It's so hard trying to be strong, it's hard being me*, I think to myself.

"You're welcome. They will be moving you to a room shortly so you can get comfortable," the doctor adds. Then he looks at Wee and asks, "Are you going to come and pick her up in the morning?"

"Yes he will!" I hurry and interject.

"Ok, I will sign your release forms and if something comes back from the lab, I will call you, Ms. Morgan. Get some rest tonight. This could happen to anyone," he says as he pats me on my leg.

"Thanks again, doctor. And please call me if you find out anything."

"No problem, goodnight to the both of you," are his last words before exiting my area.

I look over at Wee. "Thank you so much. Words can't express how I'm feeling right now. Just knowing you're here for me and you don't even know me like that."

"Terri, you good now. Rest. I'm going to get a soda. Want one?"

"No," I tell him, then I turn over and get comfortable so I can get some sleep. A bitch had a hard day.

Chapter 35
The Next Day
Terri

I'm back at home and no Rome in sight so I go to my room, put my stuff away and see a note with a rose on my pillow. It reads:

> *Sorry baby I couldn't be with you, I had to go outta town on business. I will call you later. I talked to the doc and they said you will be fine. As for our child, we can try again. Love you, Rome.*

This monkey is crazy, how do you just up and leave me in the hospital with a complete stranger in my condition at that? *It's on, I got somethin' for his ass,* I think to myself as a tear rolls down my face. It hurts so bad and I don't know how to deal wit' it anymore. I have no more fight in me and I'm going insane on the inside. I lost my baby, now I know I'ma lose him too. That's the only reason he's still wit' me, I know it. I just don't want to admit it to myself. I mean, another muthafucka had to bring my ass home!

Buzz, buzz. I hear my cell vibrating. I look at the caller ID; it's my girl Tonya. "Hello?" I answer.

"Hey, Terri, what you been up to?"

"Nothin', girl. Shit just ain't going my way. First my attack, then I lose the baby," I tell her as I'm about to break down and cry.

"What?! You lost the baby! How on earth did that shit happen?"

"Girl, I don't know, the doctors said stuff like this can happen to anyone. I may have had to go on bed rest, but he says I'm young and he don't see why I can't try again."

"Well that's a good thing. For the record, I'm so sorry to hear that."

"Thank you, but it's ok. I will get over it sooner or later, I just hope the daddy will, too."

"Oh he will. Girl, don't worry."

"Well what's up with you?" I ask Tonya.

"Girl the same ole same ole. Just another fucked up day in my life."

"What you mean, what's wrong now?"

"It's always somethin'," she spits.

"Well spit it out or forever hold yo peace," I order.

"It's Papa."

"Papa, what's wrong wit' Papa?" I ask.

"Girl, he had to go to the doctors. He say he fell and hurt his balls."

"His balls? He a'ight?"

"Well he gon' live, if that's what you asking. When I took a look at them, it look like somebody bit them fuckers to me."

"What, you think what they saying is true?"

"For that bitch's sake, I would hope not 'cause if Papa catch her ass it's a wrap."

"Now you really think Ra would bite his balls and rob him in the bathroom of a nasty ass car wash?" I ask her. I had to think about what I just said and we both said it together, "Yeah!" Then we bust out laughing. "I know, girl. Ra is capable of any damn thing, but you gon' try and stop him? I mean she is our girl," I tell her.

"Nah, she yo girl I don't fuck wit' her and I don't know why you do."

"Rachel is a lot of things but she's a down bitch. When you in a bad spot, she'll be there to dig yo ass out. Feel me on that," I try to convince her.

"Naw, she's just grimy-ass Rachel to me and I hope you can respect that on my end," she tells me with attitude. "So what's up wit' you and Rome?" she asks. I guess she is trying to skip the subject.

"We chillmaxing."

"Girl that nigga ain't gave you nothin' yet?" she boldly asks me.

"What you mean gave me nothin'?"

"You know, STD's and shit."

"Now Tonya why would you go and say some shit like that?"

"'Cause he's another grimy-ass fucker in yo life that you need to part with," she spits out.

"Now you know you wrong. You gotta respect my man 'cause the word is Papa raped that girl. That's why Ra did what she did," I spit back.

"You believe that hoe?"

"Tonya, to tell you the truth, yeah, yo man is a dirty lowdown son of a bitch and on that note..."

She cuts me off. "Ha, Ha, Ha, Terry you are so stupid sometimes. I wonder if you's a blond. Rome is fucking your so-called friends and you don't even know it. Papa would never pick me up from the hospital after somebody tried to kill my ass, then throw me a party, invite his baby momma who is my best friend and fuck her and my other best-best friend at the party in our bathroom while I'm sitting downstairs. Now that's some lowdown dirty shit if you ask me. Since you open the book, I will tell you 'cause you sho nuff need to know who you dealing with. Pam is pregnant with Rome's baby and Toni...yes, little Peaches is Rome's baby, the one you always picking up and taking all over the world. To make it worse, the bitch you just said will dig you out of a hole is fucking him on the regular. How do you think they living so large these days? Yes, Rome is supplying all they needs, not just sex baby! I know you don't think the money you give them a month is getting them Benz's and condos, do you? Check yo man's bank account."

After hearing Tonya, all I can do is cry. The tears will not stop pouring down my face. I'm shaking, scared and lonely right now. I realize I have no one in the world but me. At this point, I don't know if Tonya is fucking Rome too. After a moment of silence, I finally speak. "Tonya, I've gotta go. Thanks for the info," I tell her with a quivering tone in my voice.

"Terry, I'm so sorry. Maybe I told you the wrong way but somebody needed to tell you."

"You right, I've been slow. BUT NOT ANYMORE. I'ma see all y'all in HELL!!" I shout through the phone and then hang up on her.

These bitches gon' pay. I mean it! What have I done to deserve this? The part that hurts the most is my best friend Pam, why would she go there? Not Pam. Ok, get yourself together, pick your feelings up and move on. You got millions, you've got more money than Rome and you can take care of you. Maybe I'll move back to New York wit' my

167

parents. I just can't believe it—these gold-digging bitches! It hurts so bad my stomach is in knots. No it ain't going down like that! *All of them will pay one by one*, I think to myself while pacing the floor.

Chapter 36
That Night
Rome

I've decided to spend some time wit' Terri today. We're chillaxing in the movie room watching *Scarface*. It's at the part where Tony Montana's sister tells his man how much she loves him and shit. Terri turns and looks over at me. "Rome," she calls, tapping on my leg.

"Yo."

"When we gon' tie the knot? It's been a minute since you put this rock on my finger. I think it's time I became Mrs. McKnight."

"We gon' do it. I just wanna wait until this season is over so we can go on a nice long honeymoon."

"See I knew you might shoot that bullshit, so why don't we go to the justice of the peace and do this?"

"Terri, the justice of the peace, really? Look baby girl I want my fam to come, all of them. That wouldn't be right.

That would be disrespectful. I can't believe you just said that," I tell her with attitude, hoping it works. "Not to mention, I'm my mother's only son and the first to get married. I can't do that to her. No!"

"It's always about your mother. What about me? Can you put me first sometimes?"

"Terri, you are first. We live together, we share everything. I give you the world. How much more you want? You know how many girls would line up at the door to have what you have?"

"I want to be Mrs. McKnight, that's how much more I want. Or is it because I lost our child?" she asks with a look of pity.

I take her by the hand and look into her lovely bright eyes. "Baby, I don't want no one but you. The baby was a plus. We can try again, but for now let me make it to the top. I'm a free agent now so allow me to work my shit. You're worth way more than just becoming Mrs. McKnight, and I know you can take care of you and me hands down, but if I let that happen then I won't be the king of this castle."

"I hear you but..."

Buzz, Buzz...

"That's my phone, boo. Let me get that." I pick up the phone and look at the caller ID. "Hey, Derren," I call out, then I cover the mouthpiece and turn to Terri. "It's Derren, my PR man. Yea, oh yea...tomorrow...ok. Well, Derren, I kinda was getting married. Yeah I can wait, hold on. Terri, Derren needs me to go to Cali in the morning to do a commercial shoot. One million and royalties, baby."

"Rome, how could you?" she says, shooting me an I-can't-believe-this look.

I widen my eyes. "One million and royalties!"

"Ok, but when you get back it's me and you and the lawyer, right?"

"When I get back we can do whatever you want. A'ight, D man, it's on. I'll see you in a minute." I press the end on my cell, give Terri a kiss on her cheek and head to pack. She has attitude but she'll get over it.

Chapter 37

Pam

"Where is this man at? He told me to meet him at gate 24, now where is he?"

"Wussup, boo?"

"Boy, what took you so long? Our flight is about to take off. They already did the last boarding call."

"Stop trippin, I'm here. Your man is here."

"Yeah and I can't believe it. Let me ask you something. Why did you want me to go to Cali wit' you and not your real housewife?"

"'Cause she's sick, she lost the baby."

"What?! She what? Rome, you should be home wit' her," I tell him as we walk to board the plane.

"Ok, why don't you go to my house wit' her and I'll go to Cali by myself."

"You funny nigga, let's go," I tell his fine ass.

"That's what I thought and why you got two carry-ons, we staying a week?"

"Well if you must know nigga, I'm carrying for two." He looks at me real crazy like. I guess I got his attention now. "Yes, Rome, I'm pregnant." He stops in his tracks right at the doorway of the plane with the attendants standing by. He looks at me with his Gucci bag on his shoulder.

"You what?!" he yells, looking mad as hell now.

"You heard me. I said I'm having a baby. I'm five months along."

"I'm not the daddy. I know you ain't trying to pull that shit?"

"I never said you was the fuckin daddy, now did I?" I have to save face in front of all these crackers.

"Then who's the daddy?" he asks me.

"Rome, this ain't the time."

"Pam, this is as good a time as any. I'm listening."

"John is. I wasn't gon' tell you but since we've been spending so much time together I thought I would let you in on my secret. And for the record, no one knows," I lied.

"I'm sorry sir, are you going to board? This is the final call for flight 357 to LAX," one of the flight attendants asks him.

I look at him. "Well, are you gon' stand here and look stupid or are we going to board this fucker?"

"Let's ride," he says as he takes my bags out of my hand and we head for the first class section.

Chapter 38
Terri

Now I gotta move fast. Rome thinks his slick ass got away easy. If he thinks I bought his little convo wit' Derren, he's got another thing coming. For one thing, his phone buzzed twice. He musta forgot he don't ever, never put his phone on vibrate when he comes home. He always puts it on silent. And when his phone vibrates, it makes a long buzz sound, not a short one. So I know that was his fuckin alarm. This nigga thinks I'm a blond, but it's ok. That gives me more time to do me.

Now it's time for a sista to do a little shopping. I get in my car and drive to Penn Mar Shopping Center. I go in the beauty supply store. I buy green contacts, a two-tone blond and brown wig, some silver earrings and a blue and white bandanna. I go to the cashier and pay. Now that's one thing down. I get in my car and call my girl, Max. She's an orderly at SE Community Hospital.

"Hello," she answers.

"Hello Max, it's me Terri, Terri Morgan."

"Hey, Terri, long time no hear from."

"Girl, you still have that West Indian accent," I tell her, making small talk.

"I'm the same, just a new year," she responds.

"Yeah it's been a while."

"I heard about what happened to you. How are you doing?" she asks.

"Girl you know me, I'm fine. That brings me to why I'm calling. Max, I need a favor."

"Well what is it? You know I'm here for you whenever," she says but with a little concern in her voice.

"Can you get a hold of a scalpel?" I come right out and ask.

"A scalpel! Terri, why would you need that?"

"In light of what happened to me, I'm a little scared for my life. I applied for a gun but that is going to take about three weeks before I'm clear to pick it up."

"I understand it does take some time. Yes I can get a hold of one, but be careful because you can cut yourself easily."

"I will. Can I run by and pick it up in let's say…one hour from now?"

"You sure can, I'll be happy to see you. It's been so long, maybe we can catch up on real talk?"

"That sounds good to me. I'll see you in a few," I tell her, then end the call.

I'm so happy to get off the fuckin phone wit' her nosey ass. *Just give me the damn scalpel!* If I ain't talked to you in all these years, then I must not want to talk to you. But at least she ain't one of them that slept with Rome's ass. So she gets to live her life.

Second thing on the list taken care of.

Next thing I'm dialing Toni.

"Hey, hey Terri," she greets.

"You must've seen my number on the caller ID, huh? What you doing tonight?" I ask.

"Girl the same ole same ole, nothin. I'm just getting ready to go and get Peaches from daycare, why?"

"That's right, her little ass is in school, I forgot. I know she's loving that and all the other kids she gets to play wit'. I called you to see if you'll come over and have dinner wit' an old friend tonight. With all that has gone on with me, I just don't wanna be alone, feel me?"

"Girl that sounds good to me. I'll get a sitter for Peaches and be right over."

"No, bring my goddaughter. She shouldn't miss this, believe me," I tell her with an eager voice.

"She does love herself some Terri's cooking," she tells me.

"Can you come around seven-ish?"

"We'll be there with bells on."

"See you then. Ay...Toni."

"Yeah?"

"You know I love you and I would do anything for you and Peaches no matter what the cost, don't you?"

"Of course I do, and so do Peaches."

"I just wanted you to know that, and it's from the bottom of my heart," I tell her fake ass, however I do mean it, though.

"I know girl, and the same here no matter what it is. I'll always be there for you and I'll never cross our friendship."

"Oh really? Never...huh?"

"Never. Friends to the end."

"That's good to know. I'll see you at seven then. One," I tell her.

"One," she spits, then we end our call.

I go past the hospital and pick up my packages. I shoot the shit for a minute with Max, then I take care of the last thing on the list. I go to my boy Blue's bee farm. He gives me what I ask for and then I'm off. I look down at my time with a smirk on my face. Damn, I feel like Angelina Jolie and Brad Pitt on *Mr. and Mrs. Smith*. Shit is about to go down and these hoes ain't gon' see it coming.

Chapter 39
Rachel

"Girl, me and my baby is doing so good now. We made passionate love all night. Child we fucked for breakfast, lunch, and dinner. I just can't seem to get enough of his ass," I tell my friend on the phone.

"I see what you talking 'bout. He fucked you in yo ass, then back in your pussy and then back in yo ass. Damn that sounds good, I wish my man would do some shit like that. Girl just talking about that shit is making my pussy wet."

"I was thinking about going to Tysons 2, I need to stop by Everett Halls to get me a tux for Tonya's fashion show next week. You wanna come wit' me or do you have to stay home wit' them damn brats of yours?"

"Fuck you, hoe. My kids ain't no damn brats. That's yo kids, they eat up everything in sight and they little asses can't sit still. Anyway, I'll meet you there 'cause I got some shit to pick up as well. What time you wanna meet?"

"Let's say around three," I tell her.

"Thata work, I'll see you then."

"You know what, I'ma stop at Calista's Boutique. I haven't seen her in forever."

"Ok I'll see you there, meet me at Saks and you know what department I'll be in."

"Will do," I tell her then we hang up the phone.

Now I'm at the mall. I got here a little early so I can dash in my buddy's boutique and try on some dresses. "What you doing here all dressed like you some hoe in disguise?" I say surprised when I see Terri.

"Hell, I should be asking you that question. I thought you was M.I.A. Nobody's heard or seen you. What's going on?" she asks me.

"Nothing. I'm just spending time wit' my man. We getting along now, so that's my focus."

"Really? Well that ain't what my ears tell me."

"What you mean that ain't what you hearing?"

"Rumor has it, you sleeping wit' Rome."

My eyes get big and my heart starts pumping fast. I draw my head back, feeling like I'm gonna die. "Rome, where would you get some crazy shit like that? I would never sleep with Rome!" I say strongly, and hopefully convincingly.

"Ra, it's ok. Rome's a free man. I mean he's sleeping wit' all my friends anyway. I'm good, you gotta do what you gotta do. Right?"

I can't believe she is so calm. "So you not mad?" I ask with this stupid look on my face.

"No, why would I be? He's sleeping with all my so-called friends, but that's ok he'll get his because you and me girl, we's thick as thieves."

I can't believe what Terri is standing in this dressing room saying. She really seems to be ok with it. "Terri, I want you to know, I only slept wit' him for the money. Me and him ain't had sex in a month. My feelings of guilt was taking over me. The whole year we was fucking, all I could think about is damn I'm doing my friend wrong and she is so good to me. Now that me and my man is kickin it hard again, I'm good. You know what a sista talkin bout? T-fuckin-Ray's my man, boo."

"I know that's right, let's drink to you and T-fuckin-Ray and our friendship," Terri says, holding out a full glass of champagne.

"This is so nice of you."

"Don't thank me. This shit is Calista's. She always gives champagne to her best customers. You never get any?"

"Now girl you know I have many times," I tell her, knowing my ass is lying.

We down our glasses and talk a little about Rome. All of a sudden my neck feels tight. I look in the mirror and see my neck is swelling, my face is red and my tongue is swelling as well.

I turn and look at Terri, who is standing in front of me with this big smile on her face. "Ra, you was always allergic to bees. It took me a whole hour to get them stingers outta them suckers but now I get to see the pay-off bitch!" she tells me with this crazy look on her face.

Now I know why she is dressed like she is. Sweat is pouring from my body. I can't breathe! I'm holding my neck with both hands. I drop to the floor, trying to gasp for air. I'm trying to call out for help but I can't talk.

I'm on my back, shaking like a fish outta water looking up at Terri who is straddled over my body. "Just die already, you home wrecker! You see when you mess with the Queen Bee you get stung…" she says, and walks out the dressing room leaving me for dead. In a short amount of time I start to feel all the life leaving my body. This is all over one man… the famous Rome.

Chapter 40

Five Hours Later

Toni

Ding Dong, Ding Dong.

As I stand on Terri's porch, I'm thinking to myself, *Where is she? She told me 7 o'clock. Her car's here. Shit, Peaches is heavy when she's asleep.*

"Hey girl come in," Terri says as she finally opens the door.

"Hey to you. What in the world took yo ass so long?" I ask her, walking into her lovely house.

"*Awwwww*, Peaches is asleep. Let me put her in the guest room. Come on look at my little baby, she is so cute. I love you, baby girl," Terri coos, taking Peaches outta my arms. "Make yourself at home, not that you haven't already."

"What's that supposed to mean?" I ask her.

"Nothing. I mean you've been here already and what Rome and I have is yours too. That's all."

I go and sit in the dining room. She cooked some black ham and some black rice. Now she knows I love me some black ham and rice. One thing about Terri, her ass can get down in the kitchen.

"I'm back, and little Peaches is down. I hate she's going to miss all this," she says while getting our plates together.

"I know, Peaches loves your black rice."

"White or red?" she asks me.

"White what?" I shoot back.

She turns and looks at me like I just asked her a stupid question. "White or red wine?"

"Oh ok why didn't you just ask what wine? Damn, give me red. Are you ok? You're acting funny."

"After tonight everything will be ok," she says, holding up the bottle of Red Kendall. "Red is a good choice. That's Rome's favorite with this meal, too. I, on the other hand like white, it's pure and honest. You know what I mean?"

"Terri, is it something you wanna tell me?"

"Why you think that?"

"First of all, you're being proper and shit, acting funny. You high?"

"Toni, I can't be ghetto all the damn time, shit. We gotta grow up sometimes. Anywho, I'm happy that I'm spending time with the ones I love and love me. You and little Peaches."

"I feel you on that. We don't get to spend time together like we used to," I remind her.

We start eating and talking about old times. We are having a blast until she hits me with, "So Toni, let me ask you a question."

"Go ahead."

"How long you been fucking Rome, and when was you gon' tell me that Peaches was his child?" I start choking on my drink and gagging on my rice that seems to be stuck in my throat. "You ok? Toni, here baby drink some more of your wine. It'll make you feel better."

I nod my head up and down as water is coming down my face from choking and coughing. She comes over wit' her glass of wine and I take it all in. I can't believe she just came out and asked me that. My head is fucked up about now and I don't know what to say. I feel like a bus just ran me over or somethin'.

"Terri, who told you...I...I...I don't know what to say...I mean, I can't begin to tell you how much it has been hurting me and not to tell you. Rome and I just thought it would be best to keep you out of it. He told me that he was going to tell you after the two of you got married. So I was gon' let him take care of all that but I swear it was a one-night thing, no more than that."

"Girl it don't matter, we all fam now. The most wonderful thing came out of all of it and that is my little godchild

185

Peaches. She is the best thing that has ever happened to me. Now c'mon let's go out front. You look like you could use some fresh air. Get your glass and I'ma pour me some white. That white wine is good, isn't it? That shit cleared your coughing right away," she says, and starts laughing.

I like that she knows now. She's really alright wit' it but I still feel like a heel. This girl has done so much for me and Peaches. She has probably given us more than Rome at this point. She bought my car and my house. She gives me $5,000 a month. Hell Rome only gives me $7,000 every two months. She is really a good friend and I fucked that up being greedy and jealous of her and Rome's relationship.

We sit outside on her porch. "Let's toast to life," she says as we raise our glasses in the air.

"Here's to life," I spit.

"To life," she says, then we down our drinks and start shooting the shit about old times.

I get up 'cause I have to go to the bathroom. "Terri, I'm …I'm shit, what's going on? My head is spinning, I musta had too much to drink, let me sit back down." As I sit in the seat my stomach starts to hurt and cramp. "My stomach, oh my my stomach is cramping. Shit it hurts!" I call out to Terri.

"It is? Maybe it's the soy sauce that was in the rice."

"No, Terri. No, Terri!" I whisper 'cause I feel myself starting to lose all control of my body. I take another step and *BOOM!* to the concrete I fall. I'm feeling so sick and my head is spinning round and round. "T…Terri. Help me, please. Something's not right. Peaches, what about Peaches?" I whisper in a very low tone as she stands over me looking down. It looks like she is smiling.

She bends down and whispers in my ear, "I forgot to tell you I put Opium in your red wine—enough to knock out a ship. So don't fight it, just go with the flow and DIE ALREADY! YOU LITTLE SNAKE NECK BITCH!" She is now yelling at the top of her lungs. In a short time I start to feel cold, my eyes get heavy and I can't feel my body…

Chapter 41
The Next Day
News Break

"Hello and welcome to Fox 5 News. We have a shocking newsbreak. Two young women have been reported dead. A Ms. Rachel Heart was pronounced dead at Calista's Fashions located in Tysons Mall. She was found on the floor of the dressing room. The owner says she was the only customer in the dressing room at the time, and when she went to check on Ms. Heart, she found her on the floor dead.

"On the other side of town in Fort Washington, Maryland, one Ms. Toni Jones collapsed on the front porch of superstar Rome McKnight and sports agent, Terri Morgan's house. Ms. Toni Jones was a good friend of the two and she leaves behind a small child. Ms. Morgan states they were having dinner and drinking wine, then her friend Ms. Jones stated she was feeling dizzy and fell out. The coroner's office will send us a report on both Ms. Heart and Ms. Jones as soon as it is done. Police have ruled out foul play in both deaths. Fox 5 will keep you updated on later developments. Now back to our regular programming."

Chapter 42

Pam

"They dead! It was just on the news! Toni's dead. At yo house! And Ra! Oh my God!" I tell Rome as I jump outta bed naked.

"Slow down, what you talking 'bout? You dreaming or some'em? Who dead and where you get it from?" Rome asks me waking up out his sleep, rubbing his eyes.

"We gotta go! Oh shit, what about little Peaches? Rome, I'm not dreaming! Toni and Rachael are dead! Do you hear me nigga!?" I say to him, standing at the foot of the bed in a panic.

"They what!?" He jumps up outta bed asking again like he didn't hear me the first two times.

"They dead! I was watching the news and it was on there. We gotta go. We gotta go back home and check on little Peaches. You need to be calling Terri to see what in the hell is going on!" I shout.

"You right! What in the fuck is going on?" he says, getting outta bed now and walking over to his jacket to get his cell phone.

While he's doing that I get on the phone to make flight arrangements. I booked the next flight out of LAX, which leaves in one hour. "Rome, can you believe it?" I ask as he ends his cell call. "What happened? Did she say?"

"Yeah Ra was found dead at Calista's shop and Toni dropped dead at my house. Her and Terri was having dinner or some'em and she fell afterwards. Peaches is ok. She's with Terri, I guess."

"You guess! You guess?"

"I guess. I tried to call Terri but she's not answering," he says all calm and shit, hunching his shoulders like ain't shit just happen. I know I gotta leave this muthafucka alone. His baby mamma just died and a good friend of his and his girl, and he is just standing here talking 'bout *I guess.* This some bullshit. I wonder if he planned this shit. *Maybe him and OJ are cousins,* I think to myself. "So, who in the hell did you just talk to?"

"I called Berry, and he told me everything I needed to know," he tells me while sitting at the foot of the bed.

"OK, Rome we don't have much time. I just booked us a flight, it leaves in one hour so we gotta get dressed."

"Oh…Ok," he mumbles, still sitting on the bed.

"Rome, get yo ass up and let's go!" I tell him, giving

him a little push on his right shoulder.

"Right, we gotta go," he says, standing up.

This nigga is trippin. Even though I'm mad at Ra, I still would never wanna see her dead. Hell I'm fucking Rome and I would love to be in Terri's shoes, but dead? No, never would I want something to happen to her. I'm starting to wonder if Terri's attack, Toni and Ra's death...is somebody after me too? *Oh my God, I hope not!* I think to myself while taking a shower.

Chapter 43

Rome

I get back home scared as hell, not knowing what's going on. I park my whip and open my front door. "Terri, Terri?" I call throughout the house.

"Baby, you're home!" she yells, running up to me and jumping in my arms.

"Woo! Good, you're ok," I express.

"Yeah I'm fine. Why would you be worried?" she asks.

"With all that's happened, I just didn't want nothing to be wrong with you. When I called, you didn't answer the phone. I left a message but…"

"Well I'm fine and I got your message. I musta been in the shower when you called. Anyway, moving on. I have a surprise for you. Come with me," she says as she breaks our embrace. So I follow her up the steps to our study. "Baby, this is Pastor Murphy. He's here to marry us!"

I look at her and look at him. I'm in shock. I can't believe she would do this to me.

"Uh, hi Pastor."

"Hi son," he says, shaking my hand. I turn to Terri. "Baby, can I talk to you for a minute?"

"Sure," she tells me. "We'll be right back, pastor. Make yourself at home," she tells him. Now we're walking out the door and this lady walks into the study. "Honey, this is Mrs. Murphy, she is going to be our witness."

"Hi," I say to her while holding Terri by her arm. I could kill this fucking girl. "Why would you bring this man, I mean this pastor over to marry us, without telling me?" I whisper.

"Rome, do you want to marry me or what?"

I take her hands in mines. "You know I do, but I thought…"

She cuts me off as usual, removing her hand outta mines. "Everything after 'but' is bullshit! So all you told me was a lie? What, you got some other bitch you planning on marrying?!"

"Terri, what you talking 'bout, you just lost a friend on our front porch, and another died in our buddy's clothing store. After all that, all you can think about is if I'm cheating on you? Be for real. Who are you!? I mean *really*!"

"I'm Terri Morgan, your woman, and I don't care about all that. Right now is our time, so what you gon' do?" she asks me with her right hand on her hip.

I look her up and down. I still can't believe she's doing this, but if I don't marry her, then she'll leave me. With all that is going on with my career right now, I can't afford for her to go. My coach is talking about trading my ass and my money is low from all the bets I owe. Shit, I need her money. *Somehow I gotta make this work out to my advantage,* I'm thinking to myself. "You got me, baby. Let's do this," I tell her.

"Rome, Oh, Rome you just made me the happiest woman in the world! I love you," she tells me, so excited. But if she finds out all my secrets she may not be so happy.

Chapter 44

3 Months Later
Terri

Rome and I are married and you know ain't shit changed but my last name and our bank accounts. Yeah, he convinced me to open a joint bank account with him and get stocks and bonds together. I also added his name to my company, but we have an understanding that I run it, not him. We also signed a contract that if one of us becomes incompetent, the other will take control of everything. I think that is a fair deal since he makes his own money and I make mine. With all that has gone on, this way I know his bastard child won't get shit. Toni's mother came and got the baby. Of course you know I didn't let on that I know the child is Rome's. I haven't taken care of Pam's ass yet, 'cause I gotta let this shit die down first.

"Your love got me going so crazy right now…" That's my ringtone. Who is calling me now…? I look at the caller ID. Unknown number. "Hello?"

"Hello, is this Ms. Morgan?"

"Yes, who is this?" I ask.

"This is Dr. Smith."

"Hi, doctor, what's going on?"

"I got your test results back. I'm sorry it took so long for me to get back with you. I've been out of the country on business for three months. I didn't know your test results were on my desk. When I got back in this morning, my nurse informed me that no one has talked to you yet," he explains.

"That's fine, is this good news?" I ask him.

"Well...um, I really don't wish to break this news to you over the phone. Can you come to my office this evening?"

"No! Tell me now!" I order.

"Ms. Morgan you have cyanide in your system, very high levels to be exact."

"What! What in the hell is that? I mean, I know what it is but how? Are you sure!?" I ask. I'm so confused.

"Yes, I'm sure. The lab ran the test two times before making a note of it. I'll need you to come in my office so we can tell you what we can do."

"Ok, how about 12 noon?" I ask him.

"How about two o'clock, this afternoon?" he says.

"That's fine. I'll be there."

"Ms. Morgan, you may need to contact the police as well," he suggests.

"Thank you, doctor. I'll see you at two," I tell him, then end the call.

I'm pissed. Who could have done this, and why? First the attack. Wait! I remember at the coming home party. The fish, after I ate the fish my stomach was cramping so bad the next day. The Jell-O, I ate three weeks ago, cramps, bad cramps, that explains the headaches. The day after Rome and I got back I ate a cupcake then went to MVA. Somebody's poisoning me! Is it Rome? Nah...it can't be. Ok, Terri back-track, hell it could be anybody, but the cupcakes? Our cook baked them and it wasn't nobody in the house but me and Rome.

"Mrs. Lee!" I call out.

"Yes, Mrs. McKnight."

"Pack your shit. You're fired."

"But why?" she asks.

"Don't be questioning me. Just go."

"But it says in our contract you must give me thirty days to find a place to live before letting me go," she pleads.

"Look, I will get you a place, but I want you outta my house by the end of today. Do I make myself clear?"

"Yes you do," she says, walking away.

I get in the shower still puzzled as to who could want me dead. Then I start thinking about all the murders I've done. First Karen. Well, that was an accident. I didn't mean for her to die. Then Rachel, that bitch's ass deserved it.

Playing me. Then there's Toni. Huh, she was dead wrong, so she needed to die. Maybe it's pre-karma for all my dirt. Naw... it can't be. Shit don't come and get you for giving justice. If that was the case, everyone in the FBI would be fucked up 'cause them some lying sons of bitches if I ever seen any.

The way they did my father. He had to do ten years for conspiracy to mail and wire fraud. Either you did it or not, it's no conspiracy! That shit caused my mother to have a nervous breakdown and I had to go live with my uncle at the age of thirteen. He fucked me all day and night until I was eighteen. You would have never knew he had a fuckin' wife, the way he was beating my pussy up wit' his little-dick ass. It was a good thing meeting Mark. He was a bigtime sports agent. He was ten years older than me, but at that time I didn't care. He was my one-way ticket away from Uncle Ron's ass! I hated fucking Mark but he took care of me, putting me through school and shit. He was a good dude, at least I thought he was until I came home and found him and my mother fucking. I remember that shit like it was yesterday. I picked my mother up from the crazy home three months earlier and she moved in wit' me and Mark. I came home from school early one night and they was on the living room floor butt-naked fucking! I was so hurt, I cried for three days but I wasn't no fool. I stayed wit' his ass, put my mother out, finished school, got my first four clients, banked my first million and rolled. I never looked back. Well, I didn't have to, he was burnt alive in his cabin in West Virginia. You can guess who did that shit. Of course he deserved it, fucking my mother in her condition. I was happy when my father got outta prison. I bought him a condo in New York City and gave him some startup money for a business. I never told him what my mother did until this day. Her mind still ain't right. I vowed I would never be like her—dependent on a man. I would never take shit from them either. I told myself I would always be the Queen Bee and I would never let anybody cross me no matter who they were. That's why Pam and Rome's ass gotta get theirs, too. Somebody's gotta pay for my hurts, and when I find out who's trying to kill me, they gon' wish they never ever met my ass.

I'ma put they asses on *Ice*.

Chapter 45
Back Down Memory Lane
Terri

I just can't believe all this is happening to me. Pam and I was so close. I remember when we was in fifth grade and she asked me to copy my math test. I told her yeah and the next day we was in the principal's office. I lied and said I cheated off her. Then she said no she cheated off my paper. We both had the same answers wrong. That was so funny. We had to sit in time out for three days. We would have so much fun in school. It's still funny when I think of all the low-down stuff we did as kids, but we always stuck together. Then we met Rachel and Toni our sixth grade year. They was fighting one another and Pam broke it up. Well if she didn't, Rachel wouldn't have teeth today. Hell, Toni was beating her all in her pretty face over some ugly boy name Fufum. Even his name was fucked up! We all started hanging out together.

Then there's Tonya, I met her in eighth grade. She was in the girl's bathroom at school smoking weed. I walked in her stall by mistake. She looked at me real calm and asked me if I wanted to puff. I told her no. She was so damn fly and sexy.

"Are you sure?" she asked.

"Yeah," I said, looking down at her pussy.

"What you looking at?" she asked me, puffing on her white boy and blowing out rings of smoke.

"Oh nothing, but can I ask you something?" I said.

"Sure, what is it?"

"Why don't you have on draws under your mini skirt?"

"Why would I?" she said in a sexy whisper. Then she stood up and walked over to me. She grabbed my neck, pulled me to her and stuck her long ass tongue down my throat. I was scared and shocked at the same time, but I didn't stop her. "Lock the door," she ordered me.

So I did what she asked. Everyone was in class so it was no heavy traffic to worry about. She walked back over to me and blew smoke in my nose. Then she took another puff, smiled and put her two fingers up my skirt, moved my thong to the side and inserted her fingers into my pussy. *Pop, Pop, Pop!* is what her fingers did to my ball way up in my wet pussy. "Yes... *ssss,...Ooooh* shit." My pussy got so wet I never experienced nothing like it. All I knew was I wanted more! She laid me on the bathroom floor and placed the tip of her

tongue on my clit, moving it fast as hell. "Uhhhhh, yes!...
Yes!...Yes!...don't stop *pleazzz*! I'm cumming yes!

"Cum baby girl, cum," she whispered. I came all over
her tongue. She didn't seem to mind though. When she was
done she looked up at me, "What's yo name, cutie?"

"Terri," I told her.

"Well, Terri, you got the sweetest pussy I ever tasted
and the softest pussy I ever felt."

I smiled and got up. "So what does this mean?" I asked
her.

"This means we fucked and you are turned out," she
informed me.

"What you doing later?" I asked, fixing my clothes.

"What you want me to be doing?"

"My uncle and aunt are out of town. You wanna come
to my house later?" I asked her.

"Sure thing," she said, and from then on we would
fuck like rabbits, keeping it our secret.

About 2 months later I introduced her to the others
and we all became friends. So I ask myself today what went
wrong. My best friends. Why? Now I only have Tonya.
Damn, I hate to have to kill Pam, but a chick's gotta do what
she's gotta do.

Chapter 46

One Month Later

Pam

"Hi, girl, how's the pregnant life treating you?" Terri walks in my shop and asks me while I'm getting everything together to open up. I've been avoiding her since Rome and I got back from LA. It's something that's not setting well with me. I don't wanna think that she had something to do with our friends' deaths, but my gut says she does. I know how she feels about Rome and betrayal. I wanna have this baby first, then I can move on with my life.

I still can't believe she married him after all the women he's been wit'. I'm convinced he'll never be faithful to nobody. It don't matter. Either way, I'ma be a millionaire 'cause his friend John has way more money than he do, and he owes John for all those bets. The one thing about Rome I don't like is he's a big-time gambler and he's not good at it. I don't know how he's sending Peaches's grandmother $10,000 a month. Well it don't matter as long as he brings my $5,000 a month. Now this is the part I do not understand, if Terri had something to do with Rachel and Toni's deaths, then why hasn't she said anything to me about it. Unless… Oh my God! Unless she knows that me and Rome been fucking and he brings me money. She may think this is Rome's son I'm carrying and if she does that would explain why she's not been coming around or calling me. Here it is I thought I was avoiding her…but all along she's been avoiding me. *She knows! She knows everything! Oh shit, she's here to kill me too!* I'm thinking to myself quickly as I fumble through my nail polishes.

"What's up, Pam? We ain't chatted in a while, it seems forever. I miss ya girl," she expresses as she takes a seat in my waiting area, crossing her legs and picking up a *Vibe* magazine.

"I know, I've been busy. Now that I've opened my new club, it's taking so much out of me," I tell her, still fumbling through the polishes acting like I'm busy.

"That's right your new club, Club VOS. Hell, that's located downtown DC. I hear it's big as shit. Who would've thought, me a big sports agent and you going from a small salon owner to this big-ass club owner. Shit, I hear it's got three levels and a pool in the VIP room. You musta got a big loan 'cause the money I used to send you could never pay for all that. Or did the baby daddy pick up the tab? As a matter of fact, who is the baby daddy?"

I turn around and look at her, still holding a yellow bottle of OPI polish in my hand. "It's this guy named John. You don't know him, he's in and outta town. He's a businessman, and girl the bad thing is he's married," I tell her, trying to keep calm.

"I see, John, like John Doe. But then again you always loved messing with other people's men."

"Terri, why would you say something like that? That is so disrespectful!" I shout, now picking up my cordless phone to call Rome.

"Who are you calling?" she asks, raising up out her seat.

"I'm calling a client," I lie. I'm getting scared so I change my mind and I start to dial 911. As I press the nine and then the one…

Bow! She hits me in the face wit' her fist real hard. My body falls back into the wall.

"Bitch, you's a liar talking 'bout John. Pam, outta all my friends how could you? How could you sleep wit' Rome and get pregnant by him? I trusted you. You was like fam." She's yelling and spitting in my face.

I'm in shock. I'm standing holding my face from the pain. I don't want to hit her back because of my baby. *I've gotta protect my baby!* is all I'm thinking right now.

"Pam! So you think I'm that dumb? C'mon, you've been knowing me since grade school. When Tonya told me about you and Rome, I put a PI on y'all asses. You been

211

fucking my husband for months and you still are. I know about the checks and the money for the club. Shit, yesterday he put one mill in a trust fund for your little boy. Yeah don't look shocked, I know it's a boy. Here is the thing, that's really fucked up. Everyone knew, T-Ray, Magic and even G-man. Everyone knew but me! The three of us was all friends. I would have done anything for y'all but like my mother, my uncle, and Rome, y'all betrayed me. You know, Pam, it seems like everyone I get close to betrays me. Why is that? Who am I!?" She looks in my eyes and asks as tears stream down her face.

My heart is racing and my nose starts to sweat. I start crying from hurt and fear at the same time. So I raise up and look at her, "Terri...I'm sorry. What do you want from me? What do you want me too...*Arggghh*...Ter...Terr...T..." I mumble in a whisper, grabbing my stomach and looking down at the scalpel that she just plunged in it.

"This is what I want you to do—Die, you and your bastard child! You hoe-ass bitch!" she yells, looking like the devil is all over her face, pulling the scalpel outta me and plunging it in my stomach one more time. I drop to the floor and black out.

Chapter 47
Rome

"What the fuck is going on here?" I yell as I walk in Pam's salon and see my wife standing by her with a scalpel in her hand dripping with blood.

"What you doing here, Rome?!" she says, looking surprised.

"I'm asking the fucking questions. What you do, Terri?!"

"What you mean?! What you mean what I'm doing!? I killed yo hoe-ass girlfriend, and because you're my husband, nigga, I won't get a day for it!" she says, walking towards me with the scalpel in her hand.

I look at her with my left eyebrow up and my top lip turned up. I can't believe her. I can't believe what I'm hearing. My wife is a killer. So I do what a man in my position would do. I collect my nerves quickly. "Terri, give me the scalpel. We've gotta get outta here. Did you touch anything, baby?"

"No, I...I just...um that magazine and the chair over there," she says, sounding confused and scared as she points to the waiting area.

I go get a cloth and wipe the seats and knobs off. I grab the magazines and take the scalpel outta my wife's hand. I hate doing this but I have to protect my name. I can't get caught up in any more scandals. I damn sho can't afford to fuck my money *and* her up. "C'mon, baby, let's go. Sorry, Pam, sorry little man," I look back and say as me and Terri walk out the shop.

"Terri, meet me at Florida Ave Grill," I tell her.

She shakes her head yes. Then we get in our cars and bounce. When we get to the grill we both order coffee.

"Terri, what happened? Why? Why did you have to kill that girl? Terri, we could have talked about whatever it was y'all was going through," I tell her, holding my head.

"Rome, I know you and that bitch was fucking, and the baby was yours! I know about Rachel and Toni. I know everything, even that Peaches is yours. So don't be sitting there looking all dumbfounded 'cause you can get it too!" she tells me.

I lean forward very concerned now. "Terri, I'ma ask you something and I need the truth."

"What?" she lets out with attitude.

I take her hand in mines. "Did you kill all of them? Did you kill Karen?"

She looks around and then out the window as if she's thinking whether to tell me or not. Then she turns to me with tears in her eyes, "Rome, since I was a small child, people been using me, but no more. So the answer to your question is yes. I killed them all. Not because of my love for you, but because they crossed me. They betrayed our friendship. Now, Karen, she was a bonus. I didn't mean to kill her," she says so calm, cool and collected.

"Terri, I don't love any of them, and the baby Pam was carrying wasn't mines, it's John's, a buddy of mines. He's married and I was his decoy. The fucking P.I you put on me, I knew about him. Every time I went to the hotel to meet Pam, he was there. Pam and I fucked. I'm not gon' lie to you about that but it was only a few times. I don't love her, never did. I married you, and since we've been married I haven't touched another woman but you. You gotta believe me," I assure her.

She stands up and starts to yell. Everything goes from bad to worse. "You lying son of a shitty-ass bitch! What about Toni? What about Peaches, your bastard child? And dirty-ass Rachel? What about that bitch?! Rome, shit. You's a dirt-rag fucka!"

"Terri, sit yo ass down. People are starting to look at us," I tell her through clinched teeth. So she looks around and sees all eyes on us. "Yes, Peaches is mines and yes I fucked hoe-ass Ra. But I warned you. I told you they wasn't yo friends."

"Rome, I loved you! Why! Why would you do me like this? Why would you play me like this?!" she is asking and crying out loud.

"Terri, I can't explain it. I guess I just love women. But I've been clear of women since our marriage. I promise you, I have."

She looks me close in my eyes. "Rome, if I find out about anyone else, I'ma kill her and then you. This, I can promise you! Now what we gon' do?"

With those words that just came outta her mouth, now I'm sure I'm messing with a good and crazy bitch. So it's plan B for me. "What you mean what we gon' do? We gon' act like nothing happened and we gon' live our life together as one."

"What about the checks and the trust fund you put in Pam's accounts?"

"Honey, John put that money in my account and the mill he gave me was to set up the baby for a minute."

"Rome, I feel so bad. I thought the baby was yours."

"And you should, you just took two lives and one of them was innocent. That baby don't know where it came from, all it knew is it was coming. Now let's go home, we had a hard day," I tell her.

We get up and leave the Grill. She gets in her car and I get in mine.

Chapter 48

Six Months Pass
Terri

Rome and I are doing good. We've gotten past all the drama. I'm doing fine, my blood levels are stable. I haven't found out who was trying to kill me but I will, I just know it. Tonya, Boo, and I have gotten closer. Tonya and I never talk about what happened to the crew. I think Tonya knows. Boo had a little boy. He's so cute, she named him after Rome. Peaches is getting bigger and she's looking more and more like Rome's ass. We get her every other weekend. It turns out that Rome was telling me the truth about his friend John, who took over Club VOS. He was the investor for Pam. Pam had a closed coffin at the funeral. Her mother said it was best. I never got to see her body again. I don't understand why they had a closed coffin. Hell, I didn't stab her in the face or nothing like that. Another thing that is puzzling me, they never put the murder on the news. Now that is funny 'cause the other ones was on the news and they didn't look like murders. However, I did pay my respects. After all, she was my best friend.

Wink got 11 years; he took a plea. Boo was fucked up behind that but she is 2 million dollars richer. My business is doing great. I'm making more money than ever. I have 25 clients now, so the money is rolling in. Rome's doing better than he's ever done. He wants a baby but I told him I wanna wait. Wee's fine ass is the biggest name we've been hearing in the NFL and he's the love of my life outside of Rome. We've been kicking it for one year now and I'm loving it. Who says you can't have yo candy and suck it, too? As a matter of fact, I just left his house and now I'm pulling up to mine. Maybe I'll give Rome some of Wee's leftover nut that's still laying in my pussy.

I park my car around the back of the house so Mario can wash it. I get out and go in the house and I hear a male's voice. "Suck it! Woo, yeah suck my dick, shit yes suck it baby, suck it!" is all I hear coming outta my guest room. Now I'm feeling knots in my stomach 'cause I can't believe Rome would have some bitch in our house!

"Hey, baby," Rome says, grabbing me around my waist.

"Hey, who is in our guest room?" I ask him, feeling relieved.

"That's Berry. He brought some bitch over and I guess she got the hot's for him, so I told him to take the guest room," he tells me with his black robe on as he licks me on my ear as if he wanna fuck too.

"Romie," this bitch calls from the guest room. "Come back in and get some more of this good pussy. You only came one time. Bring momma some more of that big dickie before wifey gets home."

Now you know I'm heated. I'm pissed! Not at the fact that he fucked her, but at the fact it's in our home! I reach in my purse, pull out my .22 and—*POP! POP!* Two rounds in his ass.

"*Ahahgh*...Shit. She shot me, B man, she shot me in the ass!" he yells as he grabs hold of his ass, running around the room.

POP! One more time in his leg.

"B, B man, dial nine-one-one! Nigga, she's gon' kill my ass!" he starts yelling while running towards the guest room.

Berry musta called the Popo right away, or I was in a zone for a minute, 'cause they came without me hearing them and before I knew it I was wearing a new set of brace-lets. They took my ass to PG jail and I've been in here for two weeks now. I went to see the judge and he denied my ass bail, that bitch-ass cracka. So this means I have to stay in this hell hole until my trial date, but it's ok. I know Rome would never testify against me. I'll be home soon.

Chapter 49
Five Weeks Down
Terri

I'm chilling watching TV in the day room at the jail. "Terri
Morgan McKnight, you have a visit," the CO calls over the
loud speaker. I jump up, get my hall pass and run to the sally
port. I know it's Rome 'cause no one else has come to see
me or answer my calls but Tonya and Wee. But Wee is saying
he can't come visit 'cause he don't wanna ruin his career. But
they always tell me when they're coming. I get to the visit
hall and sit in booth eight and sho nuff, it's him.

"Rome, have you talked to my lawyer?" is the first thing
I ask.

"Damn! No hello? Shit, a brother come to see you and
all you can say every time is, have I talked to your lawyer and
the answer is the same all the time, yes," he tells me.

"Well what did he say? If you don't press charges then
I can come home. You know I was mad, I didn't mean to

hurt you. Oh and thanks for the 2G's you dropped on my books," I tell him.

"You welcome. Terri listen to me and listen good. The lawyer said even if I don't press charges the state is going to pick them up."

"What?! So what does that mean for me?"

"It means they gon' try you for malicious wounding. Your lawyer said you're looking at ten years, but he thinks he can get you five because it's your first time getting in trouble," he tells me like five years is a walk in the park.

"Ten years, five years, Rome what you saying? What about my clients? All the money we have and that's the best he can do?" I'm pissed right about now.

"Terri, calm down. I will run the business. It will be ok. Your clients aren't going nowhere. Now the worst is to come. I have some more bad news for you," he says, so I brace myself.

"I'm moving to Cali. Since you shot me in the leg, the doctor says my career is about over. One of my boys in Cali is hooking me up with a sports announcer's job on a local TV station there."

"That's fine. When I get out I'll join you, that's all," I tell him, smiling.

"Terri, you don't understand. I'm going alone. No you and me. What you did I could never forgive you for. You've done a lot and God knows I have to, but after this, I think it's time for us to part. I'm filing the papers after your trial."

"What you mean, Rome? What you saying?"

"I'm saying, Terri. . . I'm saying I can't do this no more. Don't get me wrong, your secret is safe with me. I would never put you out there like that. However, you and me is a wrap."

"Rome, are you leaving me? What you doing? Ok, go. Just give me my money, my half. I don't want anything of yours just my 15 mill," I tell him.

"About that, *uhhhh*...I paid the lawyer $300,000 to cover your trial and some is for if you have to appeal. I've got a buyer for the house as well. You signed a paper remember, we both did if either one of us dies or becomes incapacitated, the other will take charge of the finances. You do remember signing this paper?" he asks me, holding up the contract we signed.

"I remember! But what does that have to do wit' the got-damn tea in China!?" I yell at him, getting madder.

"Well I might as well hit you wit' this, I owed a lot of people. I was in debt up to my neck. I paid all of them, I wanted to clear my name before I left for Cali. I think you owe me that, T, since you stopped my career by shooting me in my leg. Terri, you're a strong lady, you'll bounce back real fast. Please don't come looking for me."

"What in the fuck do you mean, Rome? Give me my muthafucking coins or I'll kill your ass, nigga! Don't play with fire 'cause yo ass will get burnt fuckin wit' a bitch like me. Don't underestimate my ass!" I yell and bang on the glass that stands between us.

"Ta, ta, ta, baby watch your temper. Remember you're on a government phone and we're being recorded. Plus don't forget I hold a lot of secrets."

This nigga is lunchin'!

"You black no good fuck! I can't believe you would do this to me after all I've been through wit' yo sorry ass. But you know what? It's ok, do you if you ain't said nothin else. You said that right. I'ma fuckin survivor. I'ma get through this 'cause one thing for certain and two things for sho… This too shall pass. And when it do, I'm coming, and I'm coming strong. Remember me every time you look at all the superstars on the basketball court and yo ass not one of them. You's a broke down bitch-ass nigga. Who does this to a woman? Who kicks a dog when they down? Rome, fuck you!" I spit, then hang up the phone on his sorry ass.

What am I gon' do about money while I'm in this hell hole? Maybe I should take a plea and cash in on the money he gave the lawyer so when I get out I'll have something, I'm thinking as I walk back to my cell, feeling lonely as hell. But this ain't something new in my life. I've gotta stand strong. A sista gotta make it. And that I'll do.

Chapter 50

One Year Later

Pam

"She's moving! Oh my God! She's moving! Mr. Sykes...Mr. Sykes...she's moving! Can you hear me? Look at her eyes, they moved, they're blinking! Look, she did it again! You see that? Did you see it?"

"I see!"

"Pam, Pam, baby can you hear me?" a man's voice cries out to me.

"Yes, I hear you," I mumble. Well at least I try to, as I open my eyes and see two people looking down at me. I feel myself moving but I'm not sure.

"See, Mr. Sykes, I told you not to pull the cord. It's been one year and she's coming out of her coma. Aren't you happy?"

"Yes, Ms. Bates, I am."

"Pam, Oh Pam you're going to be just fine!" the lady's voice tells me as she strokes my hair.

When my eyes finally adjust and they start to focus, I see John's handsome face standing over my bed smiling down at me.

"Hi, little girl."

I try to talk but can't.

"Oh, wait don't try to talk. You're hooked up to machines so you can breathe," he tells me. Then he looks at the lady standing on the other side of me. "This is Doctor Bates. She's been watching and taking good care of you for one year now."

"Hi, Pam, it's good to meet you. I must give you some good news and bad. For at least tonight you will have to stay on these machines until I can run some tests on you. These machines do all the breathing for you, but you will be able to come off them. The other thing I must tell you is... Well... you will not be able to walk for some time. The person that did this to you....the person that attacked you, cut into a main artery, causing some nerve damage. I want you to nod your head if you understand what I'm telling you."

After she says what she says, I nod my head yes.

"Ok, good. Now you get some rest. I know it's going to be hard for you to do, because of the tubes. They are uncomfortable. I'm going to give you some medication to help you rest," she explains to me while John holds my hand.

"Pam, I'll explain everything to you when you get stronger," he tells me. Then he looks at the lady doctor funny like. She nods her head yes. John removes his hands from mine and walks out the room. The doctor starts probing me and adjusting my machines.

"Awe, there you are," she says, looking towards where John was standing. I turn my head to my right. "Pam, here is your gift from God," John tells me, holding a child in his arms.

I bust out crying—tears of joy, pain and helplessness. I can't speak, I can't walk, I can't move, I can't reach out and touch my son...my handsome son. "God, thank you! Thank you for forgiving me, thank you for helping me, thank you for giving my child life and most of all, thank you for allowing me to see another day to be able to see my child's face. God, from this day forth I give this child unto you. God, you are life, and I am grateful that you're looking over me from above. Thank God somebody musta prayed for me. In Jesus' name, amen," I pray to God. My heart is so full right now.

"This is our son. I named him Sunny because he brightened up my life the first time I saw that he was still alive. Pam, he's ok. He made it, Pam! He made it just like you, he's healthy. He was born seven pounds and six ounces strong," John tells me with a smile on his face.

I'm thinking, *Sunny... what a wonderful name*, as I smile and the tears continue to stream down my face. John puts him to my face and he kisses me. I start to love him even more.

Chapter 51
Tonya

I'm not liking the fact that today is my girl's judgment day. Terri's been locked up for one year now. At first I wasn't visiting as much because I was kinda mad at her. However, when she called me and told me what Rome did, I started visiting every Saturday and Sunday. Her mother visits once a month while her father vowed never to set foot in any kinda jail or prison again. She could call him anytime though, he assured her. Terri only has me and Wee on her side right now. Boo is still mad at her. She's saying she can't believe Terri did what she did to her brother. I can't believe that shit! After all the shit he's done to Terri, and Boo knows all about it. She knows her brother is a dog.

"All rise for the Honorable Judge Titus," the bailiff walks in and tells us. We all stand, Terri and her four lawyers as well, two of them white men, one of them is Spanish and one a black, sharp-looking woman. "You may be seated, the court is back in session," the judge, who looks like he is going to hang her, tells us. He is old, around 60 and he has all gray hair. The whole time the trial was going on, I just had a bad feeling about his ass. This muthafucka looks scary as hell. All the people on the jury are white, no blacks. *Now how is that a jury of her peers?* I'm asking myself as we sit and wait for my friend's fate.

"Ladies and gentlemen of the jury, have you reached a verdict?" the judge turns to the jury and asks.

"Yes," the old lady in the jury stands and says.

"May I see it?" the judge asks, then the lady hands a piece of paper to the bailiff to give to the judge. "Ok, what's your verdict?" the judge turns and says after reading the paper.

"On count one and two, of Malicious Wounding ... We the jury find the defendant, Mrs. Morgan McKnight, guilty as charged."

"OH MY GOD! No they didn't!" Everyone in the courtroom is gasping and talking loud.

Then the judge hits his gavel. "Order in this court, order in this court!"

Terri sits and is holding her chest, bending over. She turns and looks at me and her parents. Her mother is crying and her father is praying with his head down. I guess it didn't help that her husband and Byron testified against her. No good, bitch-ass niggers!

"Mrs. Morgan McKnight, what you did was wrong and I know you believe this from the letter you wrote me. However I don't feel like you did it out of anger. I think you were hurting. Your husband was sleeping with another woman, to which he testified in this courtroom. So I'm going to sentence you to the minimum of six years."

"*Nooooo....* Not six years, my baby!" her mother stands and cries out.

"Order!" the judge says and Terri's mom sits back down, still crying. "Now back to you, Mrs. Morgan McKnight. I too, have been in your shoes. It's hard to find out your spouse has been sleeping around. You act out of pain, and given the history of your relationship with Mr. McKnight, you should be happy he's filing for divorce. Sign the papers and free your mind and your soul. I am also going to issue a temporary two-year restraining order against you. This means you are not to come within one hundred feet of Mr. McKnight after you are released from prison. Do you understand me?"

"Yes sir, I do," she answers.

"The other thing I'm going to do is suspend two years of your sentence. Mrs. Morgan McKnight that will give you four years to do. Now court is adjourned." The judge hits his gavel again and walks out of the courtroom.

"Terri, you only have to do three years more, you already did one so that means in two years you will be a free woman."

She looks at me and yells excitedly, "My lawyers say I'll be out in two more years!" She looks so happy, but deep down I know she is mad as hell. Four goddamn lawyers and that's all she gets. She shouldn't have gotten one year. Time served, if you ask me. I know she's paying them a good ass penny. Her mother and father yell, "We love you, too." Then the bailiff takes her out the courtroom.

Chapter 52
Pam

"This physical therapy is killing me, but at least I get to hold Sunny even though I'm in a wheelchair. The doctor says I should be able to walk in a year, only if I do all the stuff the therapist tells me to do. Sunny is so fat, I love him so much. He looks just like his daddy with his cute little dimples," I tell my mother.

"Baby, I couldn't wait to see you. It was so hard faking your funeral, not knowing who tried to kill you."

"I know it musta been mom, but it's ok now 'cause Sunny and me gon' make it."

"Yes you are, and girl you better start going to church 'cause if it wasn't for God, you wouldn't be talking to me now."

"I know, mom, you're right. I will be doing just that when I get on my feet."

"Ok feet," she tells me with a mother's sure-you-right attitude. "Keep Jesus waiting if you wanna, and that's all I'ma say about that. Now what you gon' do about Terri, are you gon' tell the police?"

"No, Ma, I'ma keep it where it is. My son is alive and I'm alive too. John's divorcing his wife and we're gon' raise little Sunny together," I assure her again.

"If you say so, 'cause every time I look around, a married man is always gon' divorce they wife. So good luck wit' that. I still say you do better putting yo money on the man upstairs," my mother tells me once again.

"Ma, John's not like that," I tell her, becoming agitated.

"Yeah, ok. You say. So when can I come see y'all?"

"John wants to wait a little while longer. He don't want her to know I'm alive just in case she has a PI following you or any of my friends. I hope you understand?"

"Baby, I don't think she can afford one. Last I heard, Rome up and left her in jail and took all the money and moved to California."

"What?" I ask my mother so surprised.

"Yeah, her parents are taking care of her."

"Ma, you lying," I spit, shocked.

"No if I'm lying I'm flying." That statement is so old of her to say.

"She lost all her clients and Rome. See when you do people wrong it comes back on you, child. Didn't I teach you anything?"

"You right ma, but that's crazy! She worked for her money. That's hers, why would he do that to her?"

"The same reason why he did what he did to you. That should tell you something. A no good man will always be a no good man, so if John leaves his wife for you, then what do you think he'll do to you? You better open yo pretty little eyes, little girl."

"Ma, let me worry about John."

"Look, Pam, you see what happened when you got pregnant by Rome...Oops, did that slip? Sorry... you know how my tongue gets sometimes," she says, being funny.

"Ma, who told you I was pregnant by Rome?"

"Pam, who didn't? Be real. I'ma Christian. I'm not dead!"

"Well it ain't so! Ma, I don't wanna ever talk about it again!" I yell.

"I know you don't 'cause the truth hurts. What you doing later today?" she asks, changing the subject.

"I got to see the doctor, then I'm going to get my nails done out back by the water."

"That sounds nice, call me later baby. Pam, I love you."

"I love you more," I tell her, then we end our call.

I can't believe people was telling her that about me and Rome. How could they know? People should mind their business. The world would be a hell of a lot better. I wonder if Rome thinks this is his child for real. Naw, he's probably wit' a new girl right now living it up off Terri's money. Nothing about him will change, but I never in a million years would have thought he would do that to Terri Morgan. He had his own money, why would he do her like that? *I know he was in for a lot of money with John, but still,* I'm sitting on my king size bed wondering to myself.

Chapter 53

Jessup Prison
Terri

Knock, Knock.

"Wussup!" B says as I stand in the door of her cell while she's taking a shit.

"Damn baby, you sho know how to pick a good ass time," she says back wit' her dike ass.

"Sorry, I'll come back later."

"Naw, you here now," she says, wiping her shitty booty.

"I was just wondering where I could get some *you know* from?"

"No I don't know," she responds, flushing the toilet.

"Oh, I thought you knew every thang! Shit, I need some weed!"

"How I know you ain't no snitch, bitch? Hell, on the street you was an uppity-ass bitch. I could walk pass yo ass and you wouldn't even see my black ass," she tells me.

"B, it ain't even like that. You know me and your uppity-ass brother never got along so I just kept my distance," I tell her as I step in her cell.

"How much you want?" she asks.

"A dime," I tell her.

"That's all? Hell you ain't gon' get nowhere wit' just a dime."

"Well that's all I need for now."

"That's gon' cost you $20," she says, not even blinking.

"Fuck! That's a rip off. $20.00 fucking dollars! Where they do that at?" I ask her with my hand on my hip.

"In prison. Pay or go away."

"I want it. I go to the store on Friday."

"Thata work," she tells me, reaching under her mat to pull out a zip bag without washing her hands. *Nasty bitch.*

"Anything else?" she asks me.

"No, just give me your list tomorrow," I tell her.

"That's what's up. Ay, how Boo doing?" she asks me as I was getting ready to walk out the door.

"Fine, I guess. I haven't heard from her in a while," I tell her, still standing in her cell hoping she would turn on the fuckin water and wash her hands.

"Yeah that's how they do it. Outta sight, outta mind, but it's fucked up 'cause y'all was close. I mean anybody who lets you put a three-mill insurance policy out on they ass must be like fam," she informs me.

"A what?! What you talking 'bout, B? Who put a three million dollar insurance policy out on who?" I ask confused, as I squint my eyes.

"My bad, you didn't know? Shorty, she came to my brother's insurance company wit' the papers signed and yo man cosigned. I was sittin' right there when she did it," she spits.

"Rome signed the paperwork?"

"Hell yeah. Damn, shorty, they out to get yo ass. Well least you in here, you ain't gotta worry 'bout that shit now."

"Them fuckers! So it was Boo and Rome all this time. What in the fuck is really going on? Do you think they was the ones trying to poison me?" I turn and ask B, looking sad in the face, I know.

"Shorty, you gon' be a'ight."

"Yeah, I'll make it. Thanks, B, for the info."

"No problem. But young, don't let it worry you on the real. Yo ass gon' be safe. As a matter of fact, I'ma call my brother and let him know. Maybe he'll cancel that bogus shit."

"I doubt it, but you can try," I tell her with a stomachache.

"You know what they say, nothing beats a failure but a try," she spits, trying to make me feel better.

So it was Boo all this time trying to kill me. I wonder did Rome know. Was he in on the shit? Now I got butterflies

239

in my stomach just thinking about it. *Let me light this boy up so I can chill the fuck out!* I tell myself, laying on my bunk by now.

Chapter 54
Eight Months Pass
Pam

Now this is how I should be looking! I'm so happy I'm back to my normal size. I got so small, hell I thought the wind was gon' blow my little ass away. John still hasn't left his wife but he treats Sunny and me like we are the only ones in his life. I'm so ready to go back to my hometown. Hanging out here in North Carolina is slow for a bitch like me. I wonder what Rome is up to in Cali? Should I look his ass up and take Sunny to see him?

Nah, I'll chill on it. Shit, maybe I should take him to see Boo. She'll see it right away and call Rome's ass, then it'll be back to the old days. John's a good man but he don't lay that pipe like Rome. Rome has to have the best dick in the world. Well maybe not. I was watching the news and some guy in Baltimore City Jail got not one, but four correctional officers pregnant. Now he must have good dick or some long money one. It's probably the money. Maybe if Rome sees Sunny then…ok, Pam, stop. What are you thinking about? Rome loves Terri for real and he'll never marry you even if Sunny is his son.

"Hi, baby," John walks in our room and says with Sunny in his arms. Sunny looks so cute with his curly jet black hair, hazel eyes, coco complexion and his deep dimples. My son is going to be killing all the ladies just like his father.

"Hi, yourself," I respond.

"You ready for the trip to Cali?"

"You know it, baby. Are all my boys packed?" I ask him.

"Yes we are," he says, bouncing Sunny in his arms.

"Well what you waiting for?" He and Sunny walk through the door and I follow. I turn and look back at my lovely room with a smirk on my face.

Life is great!

Chapter 55

Terri

I'm sitting on my bunk reading *O.P.P.* This book is all of it. It keeps a sista dry on the real. I done masturbated two times already. If I can just get past the damn sex parts, they say this book is one of a kind and good as hell. I just don't wanna get past the sex scenes. I keep reading the 'rain scene' over and over so I can get my man.

"Hi, Terri, what's up?" Tracey walks in my cell and yells. Now I'm mad as hell she's interrupting my groove. My bunky is out walking and a fuckin girl can't get no peace.

"Ain't shit. What up wit' you?" I holla back.

"I got something for you. I mean if you want it, you look busy and all," she says, smiling from ear to ear.

I jump off my bunk. "Girl, I ain't got time for games, what is it?"

She starts pulling something from the small crochet bag on her shoulder. "Lookie, lookie."

"*Dammmn*, I know that's right!" She has not one, but two cell phones in her hand. "Can yo girl make a call?" I let out, excited as hell.

"Hell yeah, you know you fam now. You been hooking a sista up since you been here. What's mines is yours."

"That's wussup." She hands me the charger and the phone—my own phone! I'm about to bust a nut, now this was worth the interruption.

Tracey is standing in front of me looking me in my eyes with the her hands on my shoulders. "Terri, all jokes to the side. Don't get caught, 'cause if you do, I don't know shit, ain't seen shit. Hell I don't even know you. You'll be on your own. Do you read?"

"Tracey, you know I'm not gon' get caught and I may be a lot of things, but a snitch I'm not."

She kinda rolls her eyes at me, turns and heads for my cell door. "Yeah, Terri, that's what they all say."

"But not this one."

"Whatever you say. I gotta go. Later. I'm out. Luv ya, have fun with your new toy."

I close my door fast, put my wicky up over the small window of my cell door so no one can look in, climb back on my bunk and the first person I call is Tonya, my girl. Well she ain't been to see me in a while but she does send money every month. She says she can't take me being in here. Hell, she ain't even mailed! I stopped calling her 'cause she stopped answering my calls. She said it was too much for her to handle.

"The number you have dialed has been disconnected," the machine informs me. I can't believe it, she had this number since high school. So I try again and get the same recording. *Ok let me call her mother's house,* I think to myself.

"Hello?" Mrs. P answers.

"Hey, Mrs. P, this is Terri, little Terri Morgan."

"Hi, little bits, how are you?" she asks. She has always called me little bits.

"I'm doing good as can be, considering."

"You'll get through it. Remember, *'this too shall pass.'* I've been praying for you child."

"Thank you, Mrs. P, I need it."

"How is everybody? I tried calling Tonya but her number is disconnected."

"She's doing good. I guess at least the last time I spoke to her she was. She sends money to that Byron boy every month for you and he drops it off to me to send to you. You are getting the wires from Western Union, aren't you? They cost enough to do them."

"That's you sending me the money? Why can't she do it herself? And what do you mean the last time you heard from her? Mrs. P, what is she doing that she don't visit like she used to? The two of you was so close. She's your only child," I say shocked and wondering what in the hell is going on.

"Child, Tonya's done up and got pregnant. She had a little boy. I only have pictures of him. She said when she comes to town, she will bring him to see me."

"A child? She said she never wanted children. So her and Papa had a boy? That's nice."

"No Papa and her broke up. It's some man in California. I don't know who he is. She hasn't mentioned his name and you know me, you don't tell and I don't ask."

"She moved to Cali? What's in Cali? Mrs. P, do you have a connection for her?"

"I sho do, hold on…ok, here it is. You got a pen or something?"

"Yes, go ahead."

She tells me the number. "You got it?" she asks.

"Yeah, I got it. Look, Mrs. P, thank you for all your troubles and I will call her and see what is going on with my old friend. I'ma keep in touch wit' you now that I can, 'cause I know you don't answer prison calls."

"Yeah, they record too much stuff for me. Good hearing your voice, little bits."

"You too, Mrs. P," I tell her then end the call.

What is going on with Tonya? A son? Not with Papa? *What in the hell…*is all I can think as I dial her number.

"Hello?" a child answers.

""Hi little one, is Tonya home?"

"Yeah, who…is…this?"

"This is Terri, what's your name?"

"Peaches."

"Peaches, that's a pretty name. Peaches, how old are you?"

"I four."

"Oh my god, Peaches!" What in the hell is going on?

"Peaches, baby, who is that on the phone?" I hear a woman's voice ask in the background.

"It's a lady named Terri," she utters.

"Rome, it's Terri on the phone!" I hear Tonya yell, now recognizing her voice.

"Hang up, Peaches. Hang up the phone!"

"But daddy she's nice."

"Peach—" was the last I heard before the phone went dead.

My heart is pounding 100 miles a minute. I break out into sweats. I get off my bunk, bending over holding my stomach 'cause it's got knots in it. My head is spinning. I grab the trash can and all my lunch comes up. This can't be happening! Not Tonya, not Rome, not my only true friend I thought I had in this world! Why? There must be an explanation! So I get myself together and call again. *"You have reached the McKnights. Sorry, we can't come to the phone. Say hello, Peaches. Hellwo. Yeah, that's our girl. King says hi too. So leave a message at the tone." Beep...*

The McKnights? King? They have a son named King? No, maybe she is calling Rome King? It can't be. I start panicking and I call my mother.

"Hello?" Good, she answers.

"Mom, look Mom! I need you to look up somethin' on your computer."

"Why, what's wrong baby?"

"Mom, I don't have time for small talk. Just look this up. Google Rome McKnight for me."

"Terri, Terri baby, I don't have to, I already know."

"Know what, Mom? Know what?"

"Terri, it's gone be ok. He left you, he divorced you. Baby, you'll get another man. You're smart…"

I cut her off. "Mom, no, just do it now."

"Ok, calm down. It's done, what am I looking for?"

"Type in *wife*."

"I'm typing in wife. Oh my, he got remarried to… my oh my…Terri, he and Tonya! A picture of them on the screen with two children…I'm so…so sorry, baby."

"Mom, I'll call you later."

"But…but…I…I…" she tries to say something but I end the call on her and quickly run out of my cell to the officer's station.

Chapter 56
Tonya

"Rome, she knows. What we gon' do now?"

"Tonya, it doesn't matter if she knows or not, it's all in the media anyway. You're my wife now and ain't shit she can do. We've been on the down low for eight years. She never knew that I was fucking you the whole time I was wit' her and before I was wit' her. It's you I've always wanted. *You.* But you was wit' Papa so it couldn't happen. I was wit' her for the status. She boosted my career, then took it from me when she shot me. Now she just gotta pay. Tonya, baby, look at the people she murdered. The bitch is crazy."

"But Rome, she was my friend and your wife. Rome, I know she is hurting right now."

"Baby girl, do you remember when she was in the hospital and I came to see you before I went to pick her up? We fucked all night?"

"Yeah, I remember."

"Well, I didn't wanna leave that night. I wish I would have stayed. I would still be hooping. You and me would have gotten married. I was so shocked when you told me you put your dope boy out. You just don't know how happy I was about that. Tonya, I would do anything to make you happy. Now you got your own show and we are doing fine. We don't need any drama in our life. Can you feel your husband on that?"

"I hear you, Rome, but..."

Rome cuts me off. "Tonya, look at me. You're the only woman for me. Fuck, my dick getting hard just looking at you. Them pretty light brown eyes, your wavy long blond hair, your tiny waist, that phat ass, them sexy phat hips and them size F tits! Girl, she had to have known I was laying it on you. It ain't nothing like a mix breed."

"If you say so," I tell him and think, *Why does this man have to be so fine?*

He takes me by my hand. "C'mon now, let's make this a dead issue and go do what we love to do. Ms. Mac, please watch the kids. Me and my wife are going to retire for the rest of the day," Rome tells our nanny. We go to the bedroom and fuck all day, sleep, and fuck some more. God, I love him. But poor, poor Terri is what I think before closing my eyes to go to sleep.

Chapter 57
Terri

"Ms. Jones, Ms. Jones!" I call out to one of the coolest officers in here.

"Yo girl what up?" she answers, real cool.

"Let me ask you somethin'. I heard if somebody rats on somebody in here, say like about drug smuggling or cell phones, do they really get time off?"

"Yeah, they'll get up to one year off," she responds, looking curious. "But if you know of anything or somebody that's doing that, just don't tell me. Wait until the next shift 'cause a bitch don't feel like doing the fucking paperwork."

"Nah, it ain't like that. I was having a debate with somebody and I was telling her it was a lie about Tasha going home early because she snitched Dayton out about the food she was getting."

She looks at me. "Well, it is what it is."

I give her a fake smile and a funny look, then I walk back to my cell thinking, *If I tell about the cell phone, I might not get the year, but if I tell about the weed on B, hell I know I'll get the year. Thata put me at the door, then I could go to Cali and put them two MUTHAFUCKAS ON ICE.*

About the Author

Joy Jackson grew up in Prince Georges County, Maryland, and graduated from Armstrong High School. She attended the University of the District of Columbia. Joy is forty-six years young and enjoys writing, dancing, music, movies, family and good conversation. She is a people person who is always thinking outside of the box. Joy got into writing while incarcerated on a 12-year, 6-months sentence. She began writing poetry in the county jail poetry workshop. After finding this new talent she couldn't put down her pen and continued to write and write. After transferring to the federal prison in Hazelton, West Virginia, she discovered she had a knack for choreographing shows. She excelled at this new passion and staged shows every two months. Eighteen months later, she was transferred to Alderson Federal Prison Camp, better known as Camp Cup Cake where she evolved and ventured into the world of urban novels. She writes her second novel *Revenge Is Best Served Cold*. Her writing is dear to her heart and she hopes you will enjoy her work as much as she has enjoyed leading you through the scandalous webs of her characters. Enjoy!

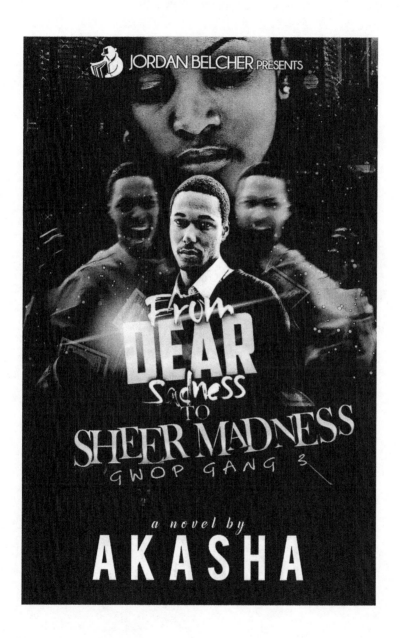

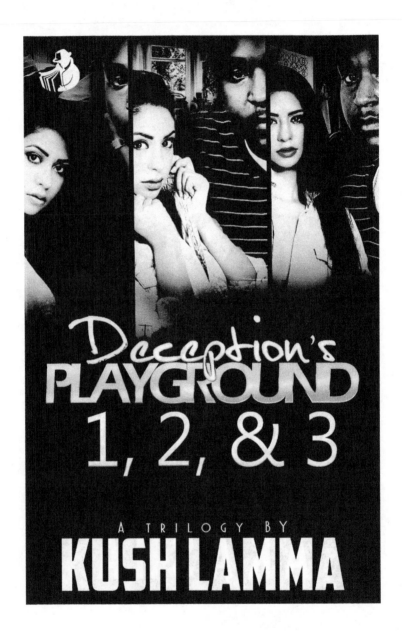

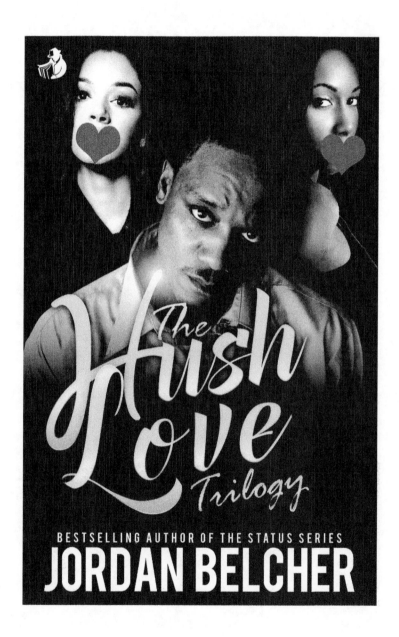

CPSIA information can be obtained
at www.ICGtesting.com
Printed in the USA
BVOW11s0723161117
500168BV00001B/92/P